Reborn

The Born Trilogy

Tara Brown

ISBN: 10::0991841190
ISBN-13::978-0991841196

This book is dedicated to the believers, you never know...
And my dad.

Artwork Copyright held by Once Upon a Time Covers
Edited by Andrea Burns and Rhiannon Nicks at Blue Butterfly

ACKNOWLEDGMENTS

Thank you to my family and friends for supporting me and believing in me. Thank you to my fans, you are the reason. Thanks to Steph at Once Upon a Time Covers!! Thanks to my editors, Andrea Burns and Rhiannon Nicks!! Special thanks to my kids and my amazing husband. In the short time this has all been going on, you have been very supportive, even when it all consumed me and you had to eat from the freezer. I am sorry about that. To the fans and the bloggers and reviewers, I bow before you. Thank you to my Nators!!!!! Best Street team/friends ever!!! Thank you to Triple M book club, you my ladies!! Lastly, thanks Dad!

Chapter One

His lips biting at my sleeve is what wakes me. I try to push him back down on the bed but he bites again.

My eyes burst open, realizing he shouldn't be here, "Damn, Leo! When did you get here?"

I grab my bow and quiver and look around. He gives me a look. He's judging me for how soft I've grown. He climbed right in the tent without waking me.

I nod, "I know, buddy." I have to remember what we've been through, not where we are.

I climb out of the tent, keeping low to the ground. I have half a mind to grab Will from his tent too, but I don't. Leo and me can handle whatever it is that's picking his wolf ass. He ran a long way to tell me about it.

Not just that, but Will will only add drama and mean stares, or that desperate look he gets that annoys me. Seeing him weak like that does nothing for his cause. I know he's sorry, but every time I close my eyes, all I see is him kissing my sister, and me strapped to a table in the breeder farms.

The silence of the forest is calming and deceptive to anyone who doesn't know about the song. But I know the song. I can hear it. A bird in the distance makes the warning noise and the others shoot it along the woods in an echo. One single sharp note. There are no other noises. No squirrels or rabbits or mice. Just the birds passing the message along the forest. If there is trouble it's always the same, this song or total silence. Either way, it's bad news.

We run along the crest of a hill and down into the valley. I can see the guards aren't in the trees. I give Leo a look. He whines almost silently and looks towards the bottom of the hill. His eyes are darting; he's looking for something.

I take my inhales slow, paced purposefully, to prevent me from gasping. "Shit," I whisper and look around; it's me and them and I have a bow. I can't kill them as fast with a bow as I can with a gun. I'm about to run back up to the camp like a coward, when I remember...I'm immune.

I almost slap my own forehead. I casually walk down the hill.

Leo doesn't get it. He tries to lead me off. I rub his ear, "It's okay. You stay here."

Their hunting party is large. I don't even understand how it's possible. Shouldn't they be dying off by now?

I sigh, pulling my first arrow and sliding it between my fingers. One of them lifts his head from the ground, where the body they're eating is laying dead. I can only assume it's the guard who should be in this quadrant.

The infected snarl at me as they lift their heads. I lose my arrow into the brown, matted head of the first one. They jump up, moving faster than I remember them being able to, and come in a mangled group. I down four before they get to me, then I pull my knives from my boots. Their skin makes a disturbing squishing sound with the slicing of the blades. Their dirty, rotten blood fills the air around me.

One grabs my arm. I cut into him but another knocks me over into the brush. Leo jumps the one on top of me but is flung across the small clearing. I hear him whimper as he lands.

I panic when I see the green blood splattering. One of them is smothering me and I don't really believe I'm immune, not totally. I'm pressing my mouth shut tight as the first set of teeth rip into my forearm. My lips come apart fast, tearing a scream across the silent forest. In amongst their high moans, my scream is so different. I feel a hand grab at my other arm as they cover me.

I struggle but a voice pulls me from it.

"Em, it's okay, baby. I got you," he whispers into my neck.

Tears are rolling down my cheeks when I open my eyes. I'm being smothered alright, but it's by Will and my blankets.

I turn my face into his neck and let it out. I don't want to. I want it to be him, not Will, comforting me. I want his fur to muffle the sobs like always as his paws wrap around me.

"I got you, Em. You're safe," he strokes my head.

I'm covered in sweat and the panic is still so intense, I swear I can feel the greasy, green blood on my lips.

I take a deep breath and he just holds me.

"Now that was a bad dream. You woke most of the camp with your screams," Anna whispers and snickers her squeaky whistle of a laugh. "No more perimeter runs for you before bedtime."

I feel for the greasy blood with my fingertips before I trust licking my lips. I'm cold and shaking, even in the heat of the night air.

I need Leo. Something is wrong. I have a feeling. Not a good one.

I lie back in my bed and curl around Will. I don't want it to be him, but it is. I know it will take me a long time to fall back to sleep. I look back at Will as I settle down, "Something is wrong."

His eyes open. He gives me a strange look and nods, "I've never seen you have a nightmare like that."

I swallow, "I need Leo. We might have to make a trek to the cabin. Something is wrong."

He kisses my nose, "Go to sleep. We'll talk about it tomorrow."

I nod and pull away from him, "You can stay, but I don't want you to touch me."

He doesn't leave. I'm glad he doesn't, but I'm even more excited that it's his choice. I don't need him.

I close my eyes and fall back to sleep.

The next morning he's gone. It's light out and I'm alone in the tent. When I leave the tent, I see the eyes of the other people on me.

Star walks up smiling, "Rough night?"

I clench my jaw, "It was a bad dream."

She nods, "After everything you've been through Emma, a bad dream is expected."

I glanced around at the people giving me cautious looks, "Do they still think I'm a monster?"

She nods, "Yeah."

My eyes circled back to her, "And yet, you get off scot-free?"

Her eyes gleam with something I assume is smugness, "It's not so free being me."

"Yeah well, you could try it my way sometime and see how different it is." I walk away, gripping my quiver.

I spend the day keeping busy. I don't want to see Will or the hateful people of the camp. I want to curl up with a good book or sit by the river with Leo. I don't think I'll be able to meet Will's gaze today, not after being so needy and breaking down.

I walk past the group of ladies I saved from the farms. They smile and wave. The numbers are less than I imagined would have stayed. I glance around the camp for the bratty babies, but I don't see them. Instead, I see the pile of dried meat is getting low. I know fresh meat is a daily thing but the dry meat is part of the stores. It's the travel food and the stuff we will eat in the winter.

I'm about to make for the woods when I see Will talking with a man. I decide to take a nap and then hunt after supper.

I wake alone and sweaty in my tent but at least the bad dreams didn't come. I grab my bow and make my way into the woods alone. Everything I do is alone. For me the camp isn't much different than being with Leo at the cabin. Doesn't matter if it's people or animals, they give me a wide birth. I wish I didn't care anymore, but it sort of hurts like I don't belong anywhere.

When I get out into the greenbelt, I miss the fur in my fingers. I love the greenery and the sounds surrounding me, but it isn't the same without him.

My dreams start to make their way back into my mind. Being in the woods isn't making the creepy feeling of being consumed by the infected go away.

I focus on the sound of the forest and slow my rapidly-beating heart. The song of the animals is like peace and quiet in its noisy sort of way. The sharp sound of the warning signal is nowhere to be heard.

The forest is still in the way I like. The animals carry on with their day. I wipe some of the sweat from my brow and close my eyes. There is fear inside of me that needs to be stilled. I force myself to be comfortable in the silence and listen for it. When I hear the hoof of something large breaking the branches it stands on, I open my eyes, pull back the arrow, and take my breath. On the exhale, I release and it's the only sound I focus in on—the sound of the arrow slicing the wind.

I like that the forest moves around me. I am one with it, even with a weapon and a dying deer.

A smile crosses my lips, it's not because an animal is dead but because nature has allowed me to become part of its natural cycle. Like I'm not a threat to it, not like the rest of us. They let me be afraid, not like the people at the camp.

I trek down the hill to the dying deer. Her legs twitch but the arrow is perfectly positioned in her side. I pull my knife and stroke my hand along her forehead to her neck. It's thick and pounding from her panicked heartbeat. I slide the knife across her throat, spilling the last of her life into the duff.

"Thank you," I whisper as she leaves her body. I'm about to gut her when I'm interrupted.

"You can take the meat without gutting."

I jump up, pulling my next arrow. An older man, with a nice smile and a twinkle in his green eyes, shrugs, "Or you can shoot my old ass."

He has nice teeth but that doesn't make me trust him. The ones with the nice teeth always fight for their survival.

I narrow my gaze, "The forest doesn't change for you. They sound the same. They didn't announce you sneaking up on me."

He grins, "No. They accepted me as one of them a long time ago. Besides, I wasn't sneaking, I just walk quietly now."

It makes me smile. I don't know why. Maybe because people with nice teeth don't usually get accepted by the forest. I guess though that I have good teeth. Granny made me brush and floss all the time.

He points at the deer, "You got a good shot on you. Lung/heart shots are hard to do perfectly."

I nod, "I know."

"You been alone a long time?"

I nod again.

He grins, "Me too—well, before I stumbled upon the jokers I live with. I just found this camp too. Who knew so many of us were gathering and living together in peace. Now if you wanna take the meat without the nonsense of gutting that deer, I can show you how."

Not sure how to proceed, I wait a moment. He shrugs and turns so I throw the knife to the ground, "You do it."

I step back and pull the arrow back, targeting him and taking a breath to steady my hand.

He chuckles, "Your arm is gonna get sore holding that on me."

I shake my head, "Nope."

He walks to the knife and drops to his knees at the deer's side.

He turns her on her side and pushes her feet together. He cuts along the belly, skinning only. He slices and trims quickly. I'm amazed at how fast and clean he is. He pulls off his shirt and lays the meat on it as he removes the hindquarters and backstraps. I let the arrow go slack and watch him.

He hands me back my bloody knife and wraps the huge pile of meat in the shirt. He slings it over his back like a filthy hobo would have before, "Name's Jack."

I nod approvingly, "Emma."

We walk back together.

"You must have been a survivalist, Jack."

He laughs, "I was a politician, Emma. There isn't anyone in the world who is more survivalist than a politician."

I frown.

He shrugs, even with the huge sack of meat on his back, "I hunted every fall with friends. We thought we were survivalists. You know, taking eighty-thousand dollar SUV's into the woods to stay in a half million-dollar cottage. We would drink and hunt and act like we had a clue." His voice trails off. He glances at me, "What's your story?"

I frown, "What?"

He grins, "You look like the other kids here but you don't act like them."

My insides sting. I look down, "No story."

"You were just born knowing how to survive something like this? Born to hunt and fight for everything you have?"

I laugh, "Oh that. My dad, Lenny, he was big into survival stuff. He owned a health-food store and all his free time was spent learning more things and stock piling."

He scoffs, "We used to laugh at those people and now look at us all. In the beginning I would have died and gone to heaven to meet someone like him."

I nod, "Yeah, he was a single dad, so when I was five he put me in day camps with people who taught us things. I learned about berries and the woods and all this." I gave him an earnest face, "Beyond the bad things, they taught us about a life like this."

He frowns, "I didn't know they had day camps like that, not for mall kids."

I snort, "They did."

"Well, 2012 was a big year for the world ending. No one ever thought it would happen, not really."

I sighed, "Lenny did. He had it to the day. Well, he did in his mind. He was off but not by much, couple weeks maybe."

He adjusts the bloody sack, "I wish I'd put my kids in camps like that."

His words burn me. I try to keep my nice tone, "Where did you live?"

He gives me another smile, "Here in Washington. I've been here my whole life."

I laugh, "Are we in Washington?" I never know where I am. I have probably never actually left Washington.

He shakes his head, "Touché."

I don't know what that means but he seems amused.

The feeling of not being wanted or liked seeps back in as we near the camp.

"You aren't that girl Emma who everyone thinks is a monster, are you?"

I don't say anything, but I know the hateful look on my face gives me away.

He sighs, "I should have guessed. The only girl who can hunt and take care of herself is the one they don't like.

My wife woulda liked you. She still might like you, 'course not in the same way. I last saw her wandering in Seattle before I left. She still looked like her. I mean, minus the fact she was a zombie."

I give him a harsh look. He shrugs, "What?"

"Your wife is one of the infected and you let her live like that?"

His eyes gloss over for a second, "I didn't have it in me, Emma. I could shoot anything in the whole world but not that woman."

I didn't understand that, "You'd let her die slowly instead?"

He nodded, "I like to imagine she's out there living peacefully, like an animal might. She's taking down deer and she's okay. She has her face in the wind, ya know?" I do know, but I can't agree with letting her live.

I grip my bloody knife and think about calling him a name but suddenly Will is there. He makes things in my stomach hurt. 'Course everything does these days.

"You kill something?" he asks.

My lip curls into a sneer.

Jack laughs, "Will, this is some girl you found. Got an arm on her like I've never seen."

Will's eyes don't leave mine, like they're searching me for something, "I know it, Jack." I glance at the bandage on his arm where I shot him with an arrow and try my best to hate him.

Jack must sense the awkwardness between me and Will;

he starts yakking again, "She downed a deer at a hundred yards with a bow and never even blinked at slitting the throat."

Will puts a hand out for the bloody sack, "I don't doubt she did."

Jack gives me a smile and Will the meat, "You want to hunt again, let me know."

I nod at him and walk away.

Will jogs up, "Carry the meat, Em."

I give him a sideways glance, "What?"

"Let them know you caught it."

I look at the camp of people, "Screw them. I don't need their help and I don't care what they think of me. They don't need to like me. I like that they fear me." It isn't all true, but I want it to be.

I turn and stalk off for the water. I need to clean up. I hardly even touched the dead deer, but I've never felt dirtier. I think it might be Will.

When I get to the water, I see Jake... of course. He's swimming and floating and enjoying himself. I want to be angry that he isn't being useful, but then he swallows some of the water and makes a face like Leo does when he's trying to get something out of his mouth. I bet he's swallowed a water bug.

When he sees me, he doesn't realize I just saw him being all goofy. He gives me his sexiest smirk, "You back for more skinny dipping?"

I make a noise that says no, but I don't answer him.

He lowers his gaze and makes a disgusted face, drawing my eyes down to the thickened blood dropping from my knife.

I grin until he hops out of the water. Then I swallow, seeing him without his shirt on, sitting on the rocks in a pair of dark-blue shorts that used to be pants. His body is dripping water. I watch it run down his tanned and filled-out chest. He looks better than when I met him, not so skinny. The eating and resting looks good on him.

He shakes his head like Leo does to get the water off; it makes the funny feeling in my stomach go away.

I drop my bow and carry my bloody knife to the water. When I drop to my knees to rinse it off, I swear I can feel him staring at me still. It makes me want to run away, but there's something I wanna know.

I glance at him, "Why didn't you tell me about it all before? Why'd you wait?" I don't need to specify. He knows what I'm talking about.

He makes an awkward face, "Em, this is a bizarre situation. I honestly thought he'd told you. I thought I was last to find out. Not to mention, he's my brother. I didn't even know Star's name when he was with her. Back then, I liked you and I thought you liked me. We spent those couple weeks at the cabin, both laid up. I'd never really talked to many girls my age so I thought it might just be us flirting. But between the time at the cabin together and then on the run, I sort of got the impression you wanted to be mine. I know it was dumb, but I did."

I feel like I should apologize but I'm not sorry. I liked him. I felt it the minute I met him.

He sighs and rubs his hands through his wet hair. He looks at me with his sweet eyes and shakes his head, "Everything's changed. It did the minute everything went crazy, and then crazier. I saw the way you looked at him, when you'd chosen him. I figured it was because he could keep you safe. Girls don't choose guys like me. You and Anna are still saving my ass."

I glance up at him and continue to scrub my knife, "I don't need anyone to protect me, Jake. I was doing fine on my own before you all came along."

He picks a branch up from the rock next to him and sighs, smacking it against the rock, "Why'd you help us if you regret it so much? Why'd you let us in after being alone for so long?"

I feel a strange thickness in my chest. It's heavy, like I can't breathe through it. I shake my head. I sit there for a second and try to find an answer.

Finally I look at him, "I don't have a reason. I just saw Anna's face, and the way she was ready to die for you, and I knew she was a person that needed to be saved. I think the world is short on people like you, Anna, Sarah, and Meg. Every town I've been to and every group of people I've come across, is filled with assholes. Men who take things 'cause they want them and women who would cheat you to be sure you get hurt before they do. I can't bear the thought that people like them and Marshall and my father get to live and be happy, but someone as beautiful as Anna might die. The minute I saw you both, I didn't want you to die."

He whistles, "Sometimes you open your mouth and stun the shit outta me."

I laugh, "Shut up." It makes the heavy feeling in my chest go away. He always makes it lighter.

I drop the knife and pull my outer shirt off. I don't care that he's looking. I pull down my pants and kick off my boots. Turning away from him, I dive into the cold water in my tank top and underwear. Breaking the surface of the flat glass-like lake is a stunning feeling. The heat of the day was intense. Even in the mountains, we can't get a breeze or a cool off.

I hear his splash as I surface.

"When are we leaving here?" he asks as he swims past me.

I shake my head, "You're not leaving. You gotta go back to the cabin and take care of Sarah and Meg. I think something is up with Mary."

He gives me a look, "Nice try. When are we leaving here?"

I shake my head as I tread water, "No, you can't come. It's going to be dangerous. I don't even know what we're doing. We have no real plan. All we have is the need for vengeance mixed with hatred." It's a line from a book I read a long time ago. A line I never thought made sense in the world. I never got vengeance before, I always took the coward's path.

He splashes me, "You have got to stop reading so much, it makes you sound like you give a shit."

I feign a hurt look, "I do."

He swims in a circle around me, "I know you do, but no one is going to believe the mean-ass look on your face if you're spouting some romantic-sounding crap at them."

A laugh slips from my lips before I could stop it. I lay on my back and watch the sky start to darken.

"Where did you go with that bloody knife anyway? Did you kill someone?"

"Yup," I chuckle and look up as the water covers my ears, making my voice sound funny in my head, "I went hunting. I love late-in-the-day hunting. The deer are lethargic and tired from the heat. Everyone always wants to do the morning hunt but the deer are like us. They wake up refreshed and ready for the day."

I don't look to see if he's listening or caring. He isn't ever going to hunt. It's just something my dad once told me. He always did a night hunt.

After a long time of no talking, I look at him, "Tell me something you remember."

He floats closer, "I remember I had a game, I was supposed to build something or maybe tear down buildings. Me and Will could play together on our iPods. He liked to pretend he didn't play when older people were there, but if it was just me and him, he was hounding me. I remember summer watermelon, so juicy it ran down my face when we were eating it. Dad said they used to have seeds. Big ones too. He said that when he was little, he believed if he swallowed the seeds they'd make a tree and he would die as it grew. I remember songs on the radio. Mom would turn it loud and we'd sing at the top of our lungs. I remember there was a girl named Becky in my class who made my stomach hurt the way you do."

My eyes are watering. I don't look at him. I just whisper,

"I remember sitting in the cabin and wondering if I was all alone. If the whole world had died and left me behind. I remember seeing my first infected. I had run and scrambled up a tree. I sat up there for so long and he wouldn't leave. A man came and he shot the infected, but I still wouldn't leave the tree. I peed my pants sitting in that tree. I stayed until I was sure he was gone... but he wasn't. He chased me but I was faster. That was the first time I discovered that just because it feels safe, doesn't mean it is."

His hand covers mine and we just float in the silence of the darkening sky.

"You won't ever forgive him, will you?"

I shake my head, "No. Not the way he needs me to."

"He loves you."

I nod, "I know." I look over at him and tread water, "I never imagined any of this was possible. It's better than I hoped for. It's better than I deserve. But it's also too short to waste on not ever knowing if he's lying to me again."

He splashes water at me, "Don't be so mean."

I grin, "I was raised by wolves, what do you expect?"

He laughs and I feel like everything is going to be okay again. I never should have let my attraction to them become something more than my friendship with them.

The sky starts to darken more and when I look up, I see Anna and Bernie walking down the path. My inner alarm sounds off but I have to stop it. I know he's a good guy. I know he would never hurt her. He's not like the rest of them.

Anna strips to her bra and underwear and dives in.

I look at the disgusted look on Jake's face and smile. Bernie waves at us, "Hey guys."

I wave but Jake doesn't. He looks annoyed.

"What's your problem with Bernie?" I mutter softly.

He looks back at me, "He likes Anna."

I nod, "I know, but when I told him she was seventeen, he seemed upset by it. He doesn't want anything to happen until she's older. He is a good guy, genuinely."

His eyes narrowed, "You sure?"

I nod, "Yup. It's Allan we need to keep an eye on. That guy's a pervert. I'm going to kill him with my bare hands, if I get the chance."

Jake laughs nervously, "You're so small, and yet, so scary."

I point at him, "Don't forget it. You're staying here when we leave."

He reaches for me with one of his bear-paw hands, "Don't think so." I try to swim away but he dunks me.

I swim away and float on my back as Anna swims up. She whispers, "I see you give Bernie that look again, and I will cut you in your sleep."

I shake my head and whisper back, "I never gave him a look. I like Bernie. I'll like him even more, when you're twenty."

Her face grows dark, "Emma, I like him now, and I'm not waiting three years to be happy. I know what I want and I could die tomorrow. It's my life."

I swim closer, "You do anything with him now and I will kill him."

She leans in, almost growling with her whisper, "I'll kill you first."

I laugh 'cause she is the only person in the world who I consider a match, "Don't push me, I have Jake and Will on my side."

She bats her eyelashes, "Don't bet on it." I know they both kowtow to her with that sweet face and nasty whisper. She swims to Jake. I see his face darken at whatever she's saying. She looks like she's crying and he stops looking angry. She bats those lashes and whispers, and he softens completely back to friendly Jake.

"Cheating little brat," I whisper, watching the display. Jake wraps an arm around her as Bernie slips into the water.

He paddles over to me like he might not actually know how to swim, "Wow, this is really cold still. How's it so cold still?"

I shake my head and try not to look like I might murder him any second, "Snowmelt from up the mountain maybe?" Before I can ask him more questions, the teenagers come. They're between Anna's and my age and rowdy as hell. They dive in, pushing and shoving and joking.

Bernie sighs. I share his sentiment.

The calm water becomes choppy as they hoot and holler.

"Hey, it's you." One of them sees me and swims over. "I dunked you last time, remember? Mark." He's closer to my age and has a scar along the side of his face.

I nod, "Hi."

He treads water near me, "You really that girl who everyone says is a monster?"

"Yeah."

He grins, "You don't look like a monster to me."

A female voice interrupts us, "You haven't seen her take down a whole breeder farm single handedly."

I turn to see a girl my age. She beams as she continues, "She saved my ass. Dragged me from the pool as the roof was collapsing on us."

I shake my head, "It wasn't collapsing. We had time to get out."

Her bright eyes flash, "No, it was unsteady." She turns to Mark again, "Then she ran us through a field with a wolf, and he attacked whatever was left, after she used two handguns and shot everything that moved."

I roll my eyes, "I wasn't alone."

Mark laughs, "You are badass. No wonder the old people are scared of you. I heard they have a name for you in the towns. Some kind of bird or something."

I sigh, "I did what anyone would have done and I wasn't alone. There was a whole team of people and Leo is like five men."

The girl nodded, "Yeah, that sexy guy, Will was there. Him and Mitch, the sniper guy. Hey, if you know Will and Mitch can you introduce me?"

Mark shoved her, "What am I—chopped liver? I got something I can introduce you to."

I'm sure I look stunned, "I gotta go." I swim to the rock and climb out. I don't know which clothes are mine. There are piles of them. The fading light of the day makes it hard to see.

I look back at the huge group of kids, people I consider kids but are my age, and shake my head.

"What the hell is wrong with them?" Anna whispers to me, "They act like the world never ended. It's like the Sweet Valley high books I read at the cabin. I expect these idiots to drive away in one of those cars with no roof and go shopping at a mall." She sighs, "We need to come earlier so we can swim without them."

I look at her, "I won't touch Bernie. You're already at least ten-years older than these people. They have no clue what's out there in the world. I can't even imagine you dating a guy like that."

She looks at them and shakes her head, "They never leave this group. They stay and make a life and that's it. They've been with them since the beginning."

I nod, "What if this group doesn't last forever; none of them has a clue. They're like the grasshopper who played all summer."

She gives me a confused look and pulls on her shirt and passes me mine.

Bernie climbs out, "We'll have to come earlier tomorrow to avoid that."

Anna grins at him.

Jake doesn't climb out. He fits in but watches me go.

That's the difference between us. He is a grasshopper too. I'm the ant who would save him, no matter what the circumstances.

I leave for the tent, holding my clothes, knife, bow, quiver, and boots. The warm, night air is considerably-less intense than the last time I was here.

I walk up the path alone and distracted. At the top, a pair of yellow eyes meet me on the trail. I grin when I see them, but they don't lose any of their worry and annoyance in the dim light.

I put a hand down, "I knew you'd come." Seeing him gives me a bad feeling. He's here for something and it makes me think about my dream. He makes a sound and walks over to nudge me. I run my fingers through his fur and hold his face up, "You okay? What about Meg and Sarah, they okay?"

He doesn't whine. He just gives me a deadly stare, like I'm in trouble for leaving him behind, or just leaving altogether.

He turns and walks up the path with me. I pull on my clothes when I get to a small fire. The lady standing next to it gives me a look.

I hate it here.

I wanna be alone and never see any of these people

again.

Anna loops an arm into mine as I finish pulling on my boots, "Let's go to the big fire." She gives the glaring lady a homicidal look and drags me off. Leo nudges her. She whispers a bunch of things to him. He makes his sloppy wolf face but then gives me another angry look. She laughs in a high-pitched and nearly-silent chuckle.

"Why do I get the impression these people all hate you still?"

I look back at Bernie who's caught up with us, "'Cause they do."

He looks confused, "You are the last person I could ever be prevailed upon to hate."

I shake my head, "Sometimes you talk funny, Bernie."

He gives me an amused look, "It was a compliment."

We walk to the big fire. It's a huge bonfire again, like last time. Only the night isn't as cool, so the heat feels more intense.

Leo sits at my feet, he doesn't lay down though. He senses the discomfort in me and stays alert. I run my fingers through his fur and hope he can calm down. I'd hate for him to eat someone out of nervous behavior.

Bernie sits beside me and Anna sits next to him, damn near on him.

He moves over, closer to me.

I lean in and whisper, "I trust you, Bernie. Don't make me not trust you. I won't interfere with you and Anna, and I won't let the boys either. Just don't be creepy, please."

He gives me a sheepish look, "She kissed me, Em. I told her she was too young."

I nod, "She's crazy like that."

Anna shoots us a look and whispers savagely, "I like you, Bernie. I like you, Em. Don't make me hurt either of you."

Bernie swallows hard but Anna takes his hand and cradles it in her lap.

The world is full of perverts and bad people; Bernie is not one of them. He gives me a look. I actually feel like he's the one about to be victimized. I fight a laugh and lean in to whisper, "If you like her, I suggest you get comfortable with her. She's nuttier than squirrel poo and you don't stand much of a chance at getting away. She's got a deadly shot and uncanny instincts."

He laughs, "Why do I feel like the woman in the relationship?"

Anna gives him a grin, like telling him he is.

In the dim light and the sparks in the air that light it up like fireflies, I see him.

He makes my stomach tighten.

He carries a guitar and sits in the same spot as last time, on the opposite side of the fire. I can't see him. But I can hear him instantly.

A girl and him start with a song he sang last time.

Leo starts to mellow out and lies at my feet. Bernie moves closer to Anna. The fire consumes my focus. My gaze is locked and my heart is lost in the broken rasp of his voice and guitar. The girl he sings with sounds sweet compared to him.

Jake walks up and sits down by Will. When he sits I no longer see him, but I hear him.

I see a guitar passed over and hear when it starts to be played with Will's.

The music is enough. It's more than enough. If we never have anything but this as an extra, surviving the struggles and the hunger and the filth and fear, I wouldn't care. The music is like blowing up a balloon at a party but the air is going into my heart. I feel fuller.

Anna nuzzles into Bernie and I see them, they suit each other so much. The flickers of the fire lights up the relationship going on between them. It's further along than Bernie wants to admit. In the flashes of light, I see another set of eyes watching them.

Star.

She smiles at me. I see something in her eyes. I can't help but wonder if mine look the same.

Neither one of us fits in, they just don't know that about her yet. I want to hate her, for the worst and most petty reason in the world, and yet I can't. I feel sorry for her in the way I want to feel sorry for myself.

We weren't born to be like these people. We'll always sit outside the circle.

The song ends and they start to sing the one I remembered Will talking about. The one with the Heys and Hos by their dad's favorite band. The song sounds amazing. Will's voice is sexy on its own, but combined with the other two and the sound of the crackling fire, I have the strangest sensation inside of me. I don't even know where it is exactly. It's like it moves around and changes things. My heart skips beats and speeds up. My stomach is in a knot, like the infected have surrounded us and I don't have anywhere to run. I feel a sickening loss of control.

I stand abruptly and walk away from the fire. The whole group starts singing with them. The voices get quieter as I walk away and I think I might have left my heart at the fire.

Leo nudges me.

I can't see his face but I bet he looks confused. I know I am. I crunch and nearly stumble to the far side of the camp as the song ends. He creeps into the woods ahead of me.

I need to leave.

It dawns on me suddenly.

I don't belong with them. The song was saying something about belonging and I don't. That's the pain and the discomfort. I won't ever be like them and they won't ever survive me. Only Leo and Star will ever make it through what we are. I feel the fire and the singing and the camaraderie tricking me and pulling me into the falseness of this place. I've spent ten years staying alive, and in the few months I've known them, they are ruining the things I was doing right.

Not to mention, I'm dragging them all into my problem.

Mine and Star's.

I lean against a tree and look back at the group; I need

her to come with me. I need to keep Anna and Jake safe. I want to hunt alone but my sister needs to come clean up with me.

"You alright, kid?"

I jump and glance over at the figure standing next to me, "I'm fine."

Jack walks up and leans against a tree next to me, "You seem edgy."

I grip my bow, "You just surprised me, is all. I need your help." I don't want to ask but it makes sense.

He folds his arms across his chest, "Shoot."

I swallow, "Can you tell them all I went back to the old cabin 'cause I forgot something and Leo was acting weird?"

"That where you're headed?"

Watching his eyes glint in the dark makes me feel like he knows I'm lying. I nod once, "Yup."

"Why don't you tell them?"

Sighing and pushing off the tree I growl, "Forget it then." I stalk off into the woods. I wish I could head back to the cabin and get Meg. She's about the only one I trust with me. The kid is a savage and filled with ruthless common sense. But leaving Sarah with Mary is a bad plan and dragging her with me to kill Marshall is an even worse idea.

I grip the bow and make my way out of the camp. I whistle when I reach the tree guards and start to run with Leo, trying desperately not to trip and fall. When I make it to the bottom of the hill, I hang a right. Instead of going to the cabin, I go for the farmhouse down the mountain.

Will is going to act like a crazy man, but if we hurry, I can be done the whole thing before he catches up to me. If I mess with the whole plan, that isn't really a plan, maybe I can keep them all safe.

Leo and I don't talk, we run like we used to. The months that have gone by haven't changed me completely. It feels like they've tried to but I'm still best with me and Leo. No matter what.

I'm pretty sure I'm lost, which is pretty hard since all I have to do is run down a hill, but I don't have a clue where I am until I hear the river. I run along it until I get to the field. Leo drinks when we reach the first place I recognize. I can't see anything, it's too dark. I listen to the wheat dancing and swaying, but without seeing, I'm going in blind. Leo goes first, staying low along the field until we reach the meeting tree. Then he circles the tree. I swing my bow and arrows over my shoulder and climb up into it. The familiar bark and the smell in the air hasn't changed in a decade.

I almost stroke the bark, it was the first tree I ever climbed, and I would hate for it to be the last, but that would be like the books I've read. It's called something....irony. It would be my own type of irony. I don't think I ever had any before, besides Will being Jake's brother. That was like God laughing at me. Jake was like seeing magic in the real world. It was an instant attraction but meeting Will was like an animal magnetism that I can't explain. I still feel it.

I sit on my branch and wait.

The moon isn't out. I think it doesn't want any part of what I'm about to do. The night is extra dark and the wind feels like change is coming. There's freshness in it we don't ever get in the summer months. I close my eyes and let it wash over me as I listen for sounds of bad things.

My hair blows in my face and the wheat dances, and just as I'm about to climb down, I hear it.

I freeze.

I don't pull an arrow, even though the thought flutters about in my mind like a moth's wings outside of a lantern.

My breath is caught in my throat when I hear it again.

"EMMA!"

How the hell did he do it?

Not breathing or moving, I wait for it. He's going to come and it's not going to be pretty.

I'm panicking when he gets really close and the light from a flashlight is bouncing around the ground.

I don't see Leo, that's bad. I don't know what to do... climb down and save Will from whatever Leo has planned, or stay up in the tree and avoid whatever wrath I have created inside of that man.

His loud steps and shouts are making me sweat. Not because he's going to kill me, that's obvious, but because he's going to draw the infected. I still hate them.

The light fixes on my face. I put a hand in the way to stop

it from blinding me.

Something scary happens. He's silent for a minute and then he mutters, "Get out of the tree or I'll come get you out."

I almost shout back but I know he'll do it. Whatever he's going to do on the ground is going to hurt less than if he does it in the tree.

I take a breath and climb down. I'm ready with my bow when my feet get to the last branch. He doesn't wait for me to touch the ground. His hand lashes out, grabbing my arm and dragging me from the last branch. He wraps himself around me. I can feel him shaking, but he doesn't move. He just whispers into my neck, "You scared me."

I don't have a response. I was ready to shoot him or let Leo eat him or just live in the damn tree till he wasn't mad anymore.

But he isn't mad.

He's loving in his twisted way. His huge body is wrapped around me, hugging me tight and bent over top of me for good measure. I can't even breathe.

He pulls me back, giving me an intense look. I look down at his flashlight on the ground, shining off to the right, where suddenly Jack's voice comes from, "Uhhh, Emma. Your friend."

Will lets go of me and grabs the flashlight. He points it at Jack who is held against the tree by a still-silent Leo.

I whistle softly. Leo growls at him once and pushes away. He circles him and then trots to my side.

I rub my hands through his fur. He never attacked Will. I don't know what that means. The man dragged me from a tree like a psycho and Leo let him.

Jack grins in the light, "That's some wolf."

I cross my arms, glaring at him, "What the hell, Jack?"

Will talks over top of us, "He has common sense. He wasn't going to let you walk off alone, Emma."

I give him a look, "I was just coming for supplies."

He snorts, "I wasn't born yesterday, Emma. I know why you came."

I glance at Jack and turn away, "You two can go back."

Will doesn't grab my arm. He walks behind me though. My skin is tensed, waiting for it. I'm going to punch him in the balls if grabs me. My dad always said, never hit a man there unless you mean it. Well, I'm gonna mean it.

But he doesn't grab me.

He follows me to the field.

Leo looks up at me. I nod. He slips into the field. I crouch, following him in. The strands of wheat scratch against me, I make the sound I always listen for when I'm hiding, the difference in the wind.

When I get to the other side I climb a tree and listen. The night is dark, except for a lantern I see coming across the field. Jack seemed smarter than to use a lantern. I sigh and climb down but Jack is at the bottom of the tree next to me with Will and Leo. I pull an arrow, "Someone's behind us."

Will gives me a look that I'm glad I can barely see in the dark, "That's Jake, Anna, and Bernie. Oh—and Star."

I sigh again, "Well, shit."

I turn and start my angry hike to the bad camp where I am going to murder Marshall, if he happens to be there. If he's not, I'm going to hunt him to the ends of the earth. I blame him for Anna's sickness. I blame him as much as anyone, including myself.

"Why you doing this now? We had a plan and a team."

I ignore him and continue up the hill. Fingers bite into my arm as I swing around, ready for a fight. Instead of him, I see Anna's angry, sweaty face. My anger falls away when she looks at me and whispers, "You bitch. You left me. You swore you would never leave me and you did."

I swallow and shake my head, "I can't risk you getting hurt, not again."

She slaps me hard and shoves me back. Her whispers get lost in the ringing in my ears. I take the minute I need to stop the rage. Everyone is tense, waiting for me to react. I growl and shove her back, "I can't hear you when you get mad."

She swings for me but Will grabs her; she kicks at me. I start to laugh, "We're gonna get eaten by something at this rate. We aren't going to find Marshall if we die." I look at Leo, he's panting next to Jake like he's watching us fight for sport. He just let Anna hit me.

Anna points at me and whispers something else I don't get. I don't really need to, I can tell it isn't good.

Will translates, "She said if you take off again, she's

gonna break your legs."

I shout at them all, "Fine, but when Jake gets us killed, or Will sleeps with the wrong man's daughter, or Bernie snivels about the hiking, don't say I didn't try to keep you outta this." I turn and start back up the hill, "Assholes."

Leo nudges me. I don't even run my fingers through his fur. I look down and mutter, "Don't suck up. You're on the shit list too." It was one of Granny's favorite sayings. I get it now. I imagine she's laughing in heaven. "None of you all listen."

I grip my bow and my pulled arrow and hike harder than I should. I know the pace I can sustain for a twelve-hour hike. This isn't it.

My legs are burning when the sun comes up. I hear Bernie start to complain but Anna shuts him up. I grin and push my legs harder. It's a stubborn, asshole thing to do, but I guess that's my role—the loner who makes everyone miserable.

We get to the guards in the trees without even taking a break or sleeping overnight, like we normally do when we hike this same trail. The midday sun is burning the flesh right off of me. I don't like to hike midday. I dehydrate and my face burns sometimes still. The first years were the worst. My skin lightens and darkens, depending on the season, so much I can look like a different person.

Will passes me, waving and whistling to the guys in the trees. He's pretty much still gasping for air.

"Hey, Will!" The guard sounds cheerful.

It's weird. I don't know what to expect but I'm nervous. I

pull an arrow and walk close to Will. I hate the way he makes me feel safer.

The camp is quiet. The people seem more relaxed. It was bustling with life and maybe a type of anger before. Now it's as if they're on holidays.

The word brings memories with it.

I remember summer holidays. I would put my hand out the window of the car when Granny was driving us to the beach. The sun and the wispy clouds would blow across the sky. I remember the smell of suntan lotion and the feel of salt and sand in my butt crack. I hated that feeling but Granny had a thing for burying people in the sand. The feeling of the cold sand wrapped around me like I was a mummy made me feel safe, like I do when Will wraps around me.

"Where is everyone?" I ask, turning in a circle.

Will growls back at me, "Not everyone is able to run a marathon in hundred-degree weather, Em. The camps slow in the summer. The assaults slow too. We don't hike long and hard. We stay low, same as the harsh, winter months. We head for the winter camp and bunk down in the houses there."

I can't believe I never thought about the fact they couldn't possibly live in the tents in the winter, not the way it is now.

I start to feel bad when I notice the burn on his face and annoyance he's trying to temper.

I glance back at everyone else. Jake and Anna don't hide their fury. Bernie gives me a weak look and Leo pants like

I've never seen before.

I realize I bullied them. I made them feel weak. The feelings inside of me are bad. Only Star looks like me, slightly burnt but not dying. The rest look like they might melt any second. Jack struggles for breath but winks at me. I don't know what that means but he laughs at my confused look.

Leo walks past me for the rain barrels. I follow him, but they're dry. A slight panic starts to hit me. I need water and my pack is back at the retreat. I have what water they brought and we found along the way. I'm thirsty.

Will comes back with leathers of water. He hands me one. I feel bad. Somehow I'm always the bad guy with him. Everyone sucks from the leathers like there's no tomorrow. I share mine with Leo.

"Hey, don't give that dog that water. He can find his own or drink with the livestock," someone shouts at me. I glance up to an angry man coming towards me.

He points at Leo.

No one points at Leo.

The man gets close to Leo, and maybe it's the dehydration, or the exhaustion, or the fact I hate myself, but I punch him in the cheek hard when he reaches for the leather of water. My hand makes a cracking noise because of the angle and the fact I wasn't really ready to smack someone around. Will has me in the air, giving me a good swing with my boot. I connect with the guy's arm, sending him flailing back on the yellow, crispy grass.

Will wraps around me and Leo stands between the man

and me. His back hair stands up. Jake runs to us, "That's not a dog. He's family."

Bernie follows, "He's our family."

The guy wipes blood from his lip, "Crazy bitch."

I try to free myself but I don't have to. I get a blur of something as the man goes down. Anna's arm comes up. Bernie grabs her, pulling her off the man. She's whispering and kicking like a ferocious animal.

I snarl after the man, "He's not a dog, idiot."

Jake is laughing so hard, he can barely get his breath when he lifts the guy up, "Run...just run..." He laughs harder.

I smile when I see the way his dark face is scrunched in the laugh. He holds his stomach and shakes his head. I feel a vibration behind me, Will is laughing too.

The people in the camp are looking at us from their tents and the forest. The few people here are confused, but the group of us ignores them and all laugh. Anna's is a high-pitch wheeze. I shove Will away as the guy flees for his life and wrap an arm around Anna and kiss her cheek. She hugs me back.

"I'm sorry I doubted you," I mutter.

She shakes her head, "I know you meant to keep us safe. But we need to do that for you too."

I could cry; I love her so much. I don't know if there is enough room in my heart for the things I feel. I don't think it's the right kind of heart. I think it's a mutant heart.

I look at my knuckles and wince. One of them looks funny, kinked maybe. Looking at it brings on the pain.

Anna follows my gaze and makes a face, "Is that broken?"

I shake my head, "I don't know. I guess." I look for the guy. I need to finish beating him for breaking my knuckle.

Will grabs my arm and spins me. He does it gently, like we're dancing like in the old movies. He's fighting the urge to start shit. I give him my bent finger in his face, "Don't start with me."

He growls, "Don't start shit."

Jake steps in the way, "Em, your finger's bent the wrong way. Come on." He grabs my wrist of my good hand and pulls me to the med tents. I watch the hurt look on Will's face and grin at him. It's my bitter, twisted, I-hate-you grin. I don't and I can't but I can pretend to.

Asshole.

Always grabbing at me and dragging me around. I lo,ok up at Jake. His dark hair and dark eyebrows make his blue eyes pop normally but being in the sun as much as we have, his skin has darkened a ton. He's so dark reddish-brown that his blue eyes shine like there's a light behind them. I think there might be a light. He is like a light.

"Stop staring at me like that," he gives me his cocky smile, "Or I'll give you the kiss you're asking for."

I look away immediately. I don't think I want that kiss.

When we get to the med tents, I see my usual doctor

right away. He gives me an exasperated look. He looks really brown too. "Seriously?" he asks.

Jake laughs and holds my hand up, "Yup."

Doc looks at it and shakes his head, "This is gonna hurt."

I sigh, "When doesn't the shit you have to fix hurt?"

Jake laces his fingers into my good hand, holding me tightly.

Doc sits across from the stump I've sat on a few times now, and pats it. I slump into the chair with Jake still holding my good hand.

His slender, clean finger gently touches all the places. He sighs, "Well, I have good news and bad."

"Bad first." My dad always said get the bad outta the way so the last thing you remember is the good.

"It's going to hurt really bad, in about...now" he snaps it back into place. I scream and Jakes pulls me off the stump. He holds me, "Calm down."

I puff and give him a deadly stare. He chuckles, "Hey, I didn't do it."

I look at the doctor, "What the hell?"

He laughs, "The good news is it was only dislocated, not broken."

It stings but I can move it. I wiggle it and stomp out of the tent. I hear Jake tell him thank you.

I stalk over to where Anna is smiling at Bernie. When I get there she whispers, "Marshall is at Bernie's, they think."

My eyes narrow, "He stole your house?"

Bernie sighs, "I think he might have. I was just telling Anna here, we should just let him have it. Who cares? I don't. It's my house and I don't care. Why do we have to go to war with Marshall?"

Anna gives me the same smile she was giving Bernie. I grin at her, "What was your response to that?"

She shakes her head, "I wanna taste his goddamned blood in my teeth when I separate his head from his body."

I nod, "Yeah, that's about my feeling on the matter."

Bernie looks defeated, "No. No. She's gotten more intense this last couple weeks. She's going to end up sick from the stress."

I frown, "Who's stressed? Besides you? She doesn't get stressed. Who gets stressed in the world we live in? There's no stress. It's live or die. We just like to have some control over whichever one is gonna happen."

I read that in one of Gramp's books. It was a civil war book. I thought it would be like Gone with the Wind but it definitely wasn't. It was more scary and harsh. I will say it suited the world I live in more than the romance ones. Although I've been finding those ones aren't so far off either. Stomach flutters and boys who kiss girls who don't belong to them, and men taking things they shouldn't, and guys who are with more than one girl, and girls always losing their senses around boys.

I have a sneer on my face when I stumble upon Will. He

sighs, "What did I do now?"

I shake my head at him and walk over to the ladies in the circle; Jake calls it the circle of doom. The Jake dog is there. He runs up, smiling and bounding all about. I drop to a knee, "Still here—hey there, golden Jake? You stayed?"

The one with the scar laughs, "Oh, he knows where his dinner is. He ain't gone too far since he got here."

I smile, "Sounds about right." Him and Jake are so alike it's frightening. I run my fingers through his fur and scratch his head. He slobbers and pants. Leo is there suddenly, giving me a traitorous look. It looks a lot like the one Will gives me. I smile and start to see the irony.

I stand and walk to Jake. I grab his arm, "Can I talk to you?"

He gives me a funny look, which I get. I never ask to talk to anyone but it makes more sense to try to be humane about.

He follows me into where Will is standing. I grab his arm, like he always does mine and pull him with no explanation. We get into the cooler part of the woods and I start to pace.

"What's up, Em?" Jake gives me a look.

I sigh, "I'm sorry for liking you both the way I do. I don't know how to not like you both. Jake you're so sweet and funny and you're actually immature for your age, which is fun and no one has fun anymore. Everyone is so old and stodgy and annoyed and tired. The world is awful in a lot of ways, and yet, you're always smiling and finding things that don't make it awful. You laugh for no reason and remember the things we had before. I like all those things." He smiles and gives Will a smug look.

I turn to face Will and press my lips together, "Will, you make me feel all the things I always daydreamed about. Granny had all those books, and when I got tired of the manuals and the survival guides, I started reading those books. They made remember things, like old movies and the way my friend's parents would look at each other. They made me wonder what it felt like to have someone look at me like that. Then I met you. You looked at me like that the minute you met me. Cocky and sarcastic and kinda mean but in a sexy sort of way. I like that. You made my heart race, before you hurt me."

I force my eyes from him, because I can't finish the most important part of the speech if he's looking at me.

I fight my nerves and my screaming brain and just blurt it out, "I love you both. I can't stop. So if I can't choose one, I choose none. I can't be with either of you. Family is more important than anything in the whole world now. If you don't have family, you don't have anything. I see that now because of meeting you. I want you both in my life and that means you have to be in my heart as brothers and nothing else. I won't come between you two."

I don't look at them. I walk away fast. Neither of them moves. I break into a run. I can't face them. I need time to let the red blush across my face and for the tears in my eyes to settle. I've never said so many things before. I never had anyone to say them to.

Thinking about them not liking or loving each other

because of me, breaks my heart. I never want Will to give Jake the look Leo gives the Jake dog.

Leo comes over, nuzzling against me. I run my fingers into his hot coat and nod, "We need to find a stream, buddy." I walk to Star and nod, "Since I'm mending fences and all, I just want you to know I'm not mad you slept with them both."

She gives me a strange look, "I never slept with Jake. He was strung out on you. When you and Will had sex he got so mad. He said he can't sleep with girls who have sex with his brother. So I guess that rules us both out, huh?"

I frown, "Really?"

She nods, "Yeah, we only made out a bit. I thought it might go somewhere but it didn't." She shrugs and pats me on the arm, "Who you gonna pick?"

I shake my head, "Both and neither. It's the only way it can be."

She snorts, "Emma, you gotta calm down. You've just spent too much time alone and you've never been around boys before. They mess with your head and your heart and your hormones. They make you want and think things and sometimes your body doesn't listen to you. Sometimes that means you make a little bit of love to a fun guy. Yeah, maybe it's not the right kind of love, but look where we are. God gave up on us a long time ago. Have some fun." She laughs and walks away.

I don't feel better. I don't dare look behind me. I know if I see either of them I'll fall to pieces. I walk to the edge of camp in the opposite way from where I left them. I pull out my knife and start to cut branches that will make excellent arrows. Leo lies on the ground beneath me and falls asleep.

Anna comes over with a bunch more. She drops them at my feet and pulls out her knife. She starts; she's slower than I am but she is getting good at it. She whispers, "You broke their hearts."

I nod, "Yup."

She nudges me like Leo always does, "You ever think that maybe they don't know how to love you the right way either?"

I give her a sideways stare, "What?"

"Who have they ever liked as much as they like you? No one." A smile plays on her chapped lips, "You just don't know how to be around boys, Em, and they don't know how to be around girls."

I stick my tongue out at her, "Says the girl who fell for the first guy she spent any time alone with."

She laughs her high-pitch wheeze, "But I've been around boys my whole life. You never have."

"I had Leo."

He raises his head, making us both laugh. She scratches his ears, "I think you think that loving my brothers is like loving a man how a woman should. But there are different kinds of love. You never know who you might fall in love with if you stop worrying so much about it. Just relax and let nature take its course."

"I don't wanna talk about it." I whittle and wonder how it's all going to work.

She sighs and I hate the sound of it, "You know Jake brought their guitars with him. I guess Will leaves them at the retreat. They're too cumbersome to carry all the way here, but Jake brought them. He's had them strung over his back the whole walk. He did it 'cause he wants to get back to what him and Will used to be. They were best friends. Will was his hero. Two goofy brothers who spent their days playing and laughing."

I frown, "I never even noticed them on his back."

She laughs, "You never stopped for more than two minutes. We aren't like you."

I feel those words.

She nudges me, "You were made to survive this world, Em. We weren't. You and Star were made to live through the bad and the worse, and now the new regime. That's what Will calls it, a regime."

I shake my head, "Maybe I can be like that fiery crow and burn up and be reborn from the ashes as one of you."

"Why would you want to?"

I don't have an answer. Not one I'm willing to say aloud.

I sigh and look at the pile of arrows. She smirks, "See, you are made for this."

My pile is huge to her tiny one. The branches she brought are gone too. I shake my head, "I feel just as lost as everyone else."

I see a tear slide down her cheek, in my peripheral. She smiles and starts filling my quiver with the arrows, "But you aren't lost. Something is calling you all over these woods. Something is telling you what to do next to make it all end. You've been in the right place and the right time for everything so far. Maybe it's like Meg says, maybe it's God. Maybe he sees what your dad did and he knows your heart is good."

I look up into the dark-green canopy, "Maybe." The image of Jesus in the room with me, floods my mind. I haven't thought about him much since.

She stands and offers me her hand. I look at the dark-brown of her skin and place mine in it. She wraps her hand around mine. Our skin almost blends, it's so dark. We look the same on the outside. I lift my bow and quiver and sling them over my back. Leo stretches and follows us back to the camp. Star comes up. Anna sighs but I smile at Star, "Hey."

Star gives me a look. I think she trusts Anna's scowl more than my attempt at being civil. "What's going on?" she asks dubiously.

"Nothing. Just wondering what the story is with Marshall."

She presses her lips together and looks back.

"Just level with me about this whole Marshall thing."

She nods, "Okay." I see a blush on her cheeks as she turns and points to a group of men, "They said that Marshall left with about twenty people. Mostly men. They knew we'd abandoned Bern's house and decided they could fortify it and take it over. It's self-sustaining. He fed the people here a bunch of lies about creating the work farm commune there. Said they would send word when it was ready for these poor saps. They actually believe him too. So we're good to fight twenty men?"

I nod, "I am. No one else fights."

She gives me a look, "I'll fight with you. Marshall trashed my brother's house." She grins, "Our brother's house."

I look at Anna, "I can't worry about Jake and Bernie. I know Will will be okay but I can't risk it. Putting them in harm's way, makes me sick. Can you just stay here and cover for her and me, so we can get down the mountain to a truck?"

Anna gives me a look and shakes her head, "I have a better idea."

I hate the look in her eyes.

It's ambitious.

Chapter Two

I knew I hated the look in her eyes. She's a scheming brat. I snarl and grumble as we make our run for it. Will and Jake were singing, and Jack, the real pain in the ass, was passed out. Anna had used guilt to get them to sing for the campfire. Bernie was chatting up another nerd about some crap to do with satellites. I don't think he even noticed the sun went down. I sure did.

We run as fast as we can in the dim light of the rising moon. It's brighter, not by much though, than the other night. Star can run like me, and Anna is too damned stubborn, not to run like us. We make it past the guards in the trees. I can hear Leo doing his running circles around us. We take turns tripping and stumbling but we finally make it to the road.

With hands on our hips and rapid heartbeats we start the trek to Bernie's house. Every one of us is out of breath and nearly dead. The run was brutal.

We jog lightly for a while before we hear it. I glance at Anna. She nods. I veer off into the woods. Star does the same but the other side of the hill. She has a handgun she managed to steal before we left. She could only hide one.

Anna slows her pace. When the headlights hit her, she breaks into a run. The truck comes to a stop. The men hop out and run her down too easily. They're too dumb to realize that. She lets them take her and doesn't fight. She makes a sniffle. It's the only sound I hear until my arrow breaks through the neck of one of them. He screams and Anna kicks his feet out from under him. She pulls the arrow out and stabs him in the eye with it.

Star shoots the other guy. The driver leaps out and I drop him. Anna runs around back; Leo is there with her. She opens the back as Star rounds the side of the van. She fires a single shot into the van. Screams fill the night air.

I run down to the van, stopping when I see what it is. It's not what I expect at all. A man lies dead with a gun in his hand. Behind him are small children. Lots of them. Star gives me a look. I shake my head, "I don't know."

"Where are you from?" she asks.

They narrow their gaze at us.

I mutter, "Gen babies."

She nods. Anna sighs.

I climb inside with Leo, "This wolf eats little kids." They scramble back into each other. I look at the disapproving looks from Star and Anna. I point, "Hurry up. Drive, Star, you know the way."

She points, "What about them?"

I shrug, "Is there a town along the way?"

She nods, "Yeah, it's a cross-town."

I shrug, "Supply towns have to have people willing to help a group of kids."

She gives me a look and slams the door. I hear her cussing. We sit in the dark.

I don't talk to them. I don't have anything to say. I don't know how to talk to kids. They're all little and scowling.

"I have to pee," a small voice finally breaks the silence.

I think it's a trap and then I remember they're five-years old. "Bang on the wall behind you all. She'll stop the truck."

One of them thumps and the truck skids to a stop. I hear the driver's door and then squint as the light blinds me. It makes me scared when I see the light. Bad memories flood my mind. Instead of terror and survival staring me in the face, I see Star giving me a shitty look.

"They gotta pee."

She rolls her eyes, "Let's go, make it fast." She clearly likes kids as much as I do. I like one kid in the whole world. One little blonde.

Star points at them when they don't budge, "We saved you from the bad guys. We're going to free you so you can find your moms again."

One kid makes a snarl-like cat noise. It's almost like a hiss. I climb out and pat my hand against my thigh. Leo follows me out and then they leave, hesitantly.

I give her a grim look, "Forgot I told them he eats kids."

She laughs, "Oh yeah."

They run into the bushes. We stand there until we hear the passenger door. Anna gives us a look. I frown, "What?"

She walks over and points at the bushes, "They ran away—seriously. You going to stand here all day?"

I look at the woods, confused, "Well, I guess that was probably what I woulda done."

Star nods, "Yup."

I don't know what to do. They're little kids alone in the woods. I glance at Star, "Should we go get them?"

She shrugs, "I don't know."

We wait a few minutes and I shake my head, "Let's go. We won't be doing them any favors if we go drag them from the woods." I take the lazy, coward's path. I don't want a dozen children to take care of.

Star nods but Anna looks confused, "Leave them?"

"Yes!" I climb back into the back of the truck and close the doors again. I hear Star start it and then we drive for what feels like forever. I'm passed out in the back, leaning on Leo, when the truck makes a weird stop. Anna opens the door, "Out of gas," she whispers.

I yawn and grab my bow and quiver. We stretch and sit on the back of the truck, eating the dried meats we stole.

"You worried about this?" I ask.

Star looks at the road and sighs, "Nope."

Anna gives me a cautionary look.

"Why not?"

She grins over at me, "Because Bern has a giant weapons store for just this moment. It's in the woods, down the bomb path."

"The bomb path?"

She laughs, "I know the way through."

That doesn't make me feel better.

We walk until I feel sick. I can't imagine how Anna feels. I pull an arrow, "Go find some water to refill the skins and I'll find some dinner. Anna, make a fire and a spit."

They leave in opposite directions. They will never like each other. I can't even imagine how uncomfortable it was in the front seat. I'm grateful I sat in the back with the weird little kids. Leo and I hike for a few minutes before I find a good tree. I press my body against it and wait. I close my eyes to listen.

I hear a branch break. It doesn't sound huge, but when I look for the animal, I'm excited to see a massive hare. I haven't had hare since Jake dang near killed us by under cooking it.

I pull back the arrow, lining it up. I feel the wind on my face and take a breath. When I release the arrow, it misses. I frown and pull another as the hare tries to hop away. I hit him in the neck. Leo pounces, grabbing him and giving him the death shake. I skin and gut him quick, wondering if the gutless cleaning works on hares too?

I get back to the fire with some leaves filled with berries I know we can eat.

Anna is holding up roots. She smiles, "They taste like potatoes." I just catch her whisper over the crackle of the fire.

Star comes with full skins. She sighs, "I am starving."

Anna puts the hare on the spit and turns him slowly. Star mashes the berries on the broad leaf. She swears if we rub it on the cooked hare it'll taste better. I tie the roots into one of the huge broad leaves with vine. The vine cooks slowly, allowing the leaf to steam the roots.

"That smells good," I mutter.

Anna smiles and continues to slowly turn the hare. I pull the roots out of the ashes with my boot and let them cool for a few minutes. Star grabs more huge leaves. We're so hungry we don't notice that no one talks. We tear the fur from the cooling carcass and drag each bite through the mashed berries. I moan into my bites and Anna wheezes. Star nods, "I told you."

I laugh and eat a bite of the root. It does taste like potatoes. I give Leo a bite, he chews and walks away. We all laugh, "Guess he doesn't like the berries."

"More for us."

I'm stuffed when I finish off the water in my skin.

Star yawns, "Normally, I'd be too full to sleep but shit I'm beat."

Anna's eyes are closing, even though she's sitting up. I nudge her with my boot, "Sleep."

She nods and gets up. I put more wood on the fire just as Leo finds his way back. He's licking his chops and has, no doubt, also had a feast of his own making.

We pull boughs and make a bed. The three of us sleep next to each other. I know Leo keeps guard. He always does when we're out like this. I think it's why he likes the cabin so much, he sleeps the whole time.

We start back on the road in the morning, eating our stolen, dried meats and the last of the berries. When we get to a spot on the road, Star points, "This way." She heads into the brush, but I don't see a marker. We cross a field when we get past the initial brush. I see jagged remains of buildings over top of the trees at the other side.

"Used to be my soccer field when I was little," she whispers.

Anna and I give her a look, "You lived near here?" I ask.

She nods, "There used to be buildings and things. It was a fancy neighborhood, just down here." We crest a hill and stop. My skin crawls seeing it. It isn't the first crater I've seen.

"Was it nuclear?"

She shrugs her head, "Not a clue. Bern said it was a hydrogen bomb."

I nod, "That's a nuclear bomb. We shouldn't be here. Lenny said twenty years."

But we don't move. We stand on the edge of the massive crater and just look.

Finally, Anna whispers, "I think I can feel the dead in the air."

I nod, "It's creepy." I've avoided craters my whole life.

Leo is anxious. He doesn't like it. I follow him out, hoping they'll follow me and we won't ever have to come back this way again.

We walk to a new road.

"How do you remember this so well?"

Star looks over at me, "I've walked it a lot."

I frown, "Why wouldn't you get him to drive you?"

Her eyes twinkle, "Trucks make noise. I don't like making noise."

We are more alike than I have realized.

She stops on the road and looks, "This is the bomb path. Stay directly behind me the entire time." She cuts into the woods. My feet are hurting and my legs are exhausted. I can't imagine how Anna feels.

I step where Anna steps as she follows Star in. The brush is dense.

I hold Leo by the scruff and force him to follow my steps. He gets it after a minute and stays in the line.

Star drops to her knees after a while, lifting a huge piece of the land up. It's a thin, metal sheet with dirt and moss stuck to the top of it. Inside is a small shelter loaded with guns and food. She jumps down and passes me a package. I open it and start to eat, too fast. I gobble back the nuts and seeds. Anna is wolfing down a bar. I take a protein bar and start on it at the same time as the nuts. Star is pouring a package into her throat. She's chewing fast too. She passes us water bottles. The three of us gorge. I don't stop myself. It's been lean rations for days. I sit and sigh as it hits my belly with a thud.

"I need to go the bathroom." Anna makes a face.

I laugh. Star passes her a tissue packet. Anna's face breaks into a huge smile, "No leaves!"

Star laughs with me, "Can you remember the path back?"

Anna nods and starts back the way we came.

"Bernie thought of everything."

She nods, "He really did. He set this up as a bit of a fallout shelter. It was in case the house got over taken. He is a smart guy. Not to mention, he had the list."

I frown, "The list?"

She nods, "Yeah. They were all given a list—the higher ups and the necessary people."

My stomach sinks, "So only certain people would survive." I can't help but think about the lady who saved me in the town, when the others were looking for me. In a sick way I have to be happy that she was able to save me, so I could save Jake.

Anna comes back frowning, minus the tissue. I smile, I know she hates going to the bathroom in the woods. Leo trots after her. She looks back at him, giving him a disgusted look. I know what he's done. I hate it too, but he feels the need to clean up the evidence from his family. It's his nature. I hadn't even noticed he'd followed her.

Star sighs, "Well, let's do this then." She passes me two handguns, leather straps, and four clips. I load a clip in each shiny, silver gun. She straps the leathers around my thighs and places the clips in them. My jaw drops, "That's cool."

She nods, "I know." She pulls out two sniper rifles and passes one to Anna with a belt of ammo. Anna grins, "Best day ever. All that friggin' walking was worth it." She shoots a glare at Leo, "Well, except for that. That was nasty."

I roll my eyes.

Leo whines as he finishes his protein bar. I pour a bottle of water and he drinks from the stream. I pat his head, "You ready?"

He finishes the water and yawns.

I drop my bow and arrow into the hole for safekeeping. I'll always choose a gun over a bow.

She climbs out of the hole and slaps the lid back down. She turns something I never noticed before and covers it with moss again.

She puts a finger to her lips. I nod.

We walk in a line. They can't fight, not like I can, but they can both shoot like marksmen.

I see the house after we walk for a bit. I see a man in a tree and stop. Star shoots him out of the tree with the silencer on. I love silencers. He falls, making a huge ruckus, and drops to the ground with a thud. His face is slack. When we walk past him, I take his rifle and sling it onto my back.

The closer we get, the more we hear. They're building or fixing the mess they've made, when they trashed the house.

Anna's face is savage, as usual. Star stops us and turns, "From here on out there are no bombs in the woods. Don't backtrack though. Anna, stay in the trees, no matter what."

Anna points to a tree and nods once. She walks there,

climbing it. If I look carefully, I can see movement. Star takes the left side and gives me a grin, "Good luck."

I nod.

My stomach is filled with nerves, but the possibility I will see Marshall suffer is driving me on. The need for vengeance is like a magic pill. I have more cunning and energy than I could have imagined.

I slip from the woods, and scan the grass. There are men everywhere. They're moving crates and fixing things, like the front door. I don't see Marshall.

A man's face lifts from a box. He opens his mouth to scream but he drops to the ground dead. Anna.

I smile and creep across the expansive field. I point my gun to shoot a man walking with a rifle, but he falls dead. They are dropping like flies, silently. Finally, as one falls, another opens his mouth, "WE ARE BEING ATTACKED!"

I shoot him, making the first real gunshot ring through the air. At least half of the twenty are dead now.

My heart is beating in my throat, Leo nudges me constantly. I place my back against the siding of the house as I hear the shots firing. All I can do is pray Anna and Star manage to move before a scope reflection gets them killed.

I slide along the house to the side door. I glance in the window once. Nothing.

I open the door and let Leo inside. He growls and snarls inside of a doorway to the right. I step into the room and shoot the man aiming at Leo, who is devouring someone on the floor.

We walk together through the house, checking rooms. Someone grabs me from behind. I feel a knife slice across my arm, when I block the grip on my throat. Leo dives, taking us both to the ground. His face is rage and red froth when his huge jaw snaps at the head behind me. I not only hear his teeth sink into the flesh, but I also feel the breaking of bone. I shudder and stand. My arm is pouring blood. I rip the bottom off my shirt and make a bandage. I wrap it tightly and continue on. Leo looks worried but I give him a stern look. He walks ahead.

I hear a sound behind me. Turning with my gun ready, I see Star grinning.

We sneak through the house. I hear talking and peek my head around the corner. It's a man I recognize whispering to two other men.

They're all very large, close and heavily armed. I sigh softly and look at Leo; he can't come in there. I nod back behind us. He makes a face. I give him my alpha look. He bows his head and backs up. I jump out, shooting the man whispering, in the head. I shoot the second man, but the third man has his gun on me fast. His finger jerks at the trigger but he drops on his back and shoots the ceiling. I look back at Star. She winks. She leaps in front of me, rifle out. I see her finger pull the trigger once before we are in the kitchen. It's a mess.

"Bernie's going to be pissed," she mutters and looks around, "They're in the cellar."

I frown, "We can't get in there, can we?"

Her smile tells me I'm wrong when she looks back at me.

A noise from behind us scares me. I slip against the wall,

ready but Anna walks in, out of breath and whispering like a mad woman.

I step closer to hear her better. She points, "They're here."

My stomach clenches, "Will and Jake?"

She nods and tries to catch her breath.

"Did they see you?"

She shakes her head and gives me a look. I smirk until I see the blood trickling down her arm. I grab at it but she slaps my hand away, "Bullet grazed me. It's a scratch."

I sigh, "People die from scratches."

She rolls her eyes.

Star drops to her knees and fishes something out from under the sink. She passes me her gun and stands up with a round thing in her hands.

She holds it up, "When I open the door, you press this on the side and toss it inside of the cellar."

I nod. I don't feel good. I have a bad feeling. I take the round thing; it looks like a grenade. I've seen them once. It was in an old military compound where I found my silencer.

I stare at the black button that I have to press and nod, "Let's do this."

Leo whines. He sniffs the food a bit and circles. I scratch his head. We walk to the cellar. Anna stays at the top of the stars with her gun ready. Star punches something into the keypad. A beep breaks the silence. I almost jump. She puts her hand on the handle and nods. She pulls back fast, I press the button and toss it inside. Instantly, smoke fills the room. She slams the door shut. I look up at Anna but she's gone.

"Trap."

Leo is gone too. I run up the stairs, knowing the cellar is empty. Marshall is smarter than that.

I round the corner from the kitchen and come to a skidding stop. Through the doorway I see a blonde head. A desperate cry makes an attempt from my throat but the fear has it clogged up. Next to the blonde head is a snarling and savage-looking teenager. I stuff the guns in the back of my pants quickly and hold the rifle like it's my only weapon. I stumble out onto the front porch. Leo is huge, his hair is standing on end. A large man is holding Anna with a gun to her throat.

I look back at Star. Her eyes don't show anything. I don't know if it's her that's betrayed us, but I suspect. I know I've spent my life on the coward's path and she is my sister. We share the same pathetic blood.

I grip my rifle, walking forward.

Marshall clasps his hands, "Why there she is. The star of our party."

I cringe; it was Star all along. The van that drove up wasn't Jake and Will. It was Marshall. He never was at Bernie's house. He was walking to my cabin to steal my family. I fake a smile at Sarah but she doesn't buy it. I nod at Meg. She snarls and claws at the hand holding her.

"Give us your weapons and surrender and they live. Fight

me and they die."

I drop the rifle instantly and shoot Leo a sideways glance. He bows his head. As I walk forward, he will retreat to the side of the house. He will run into the woods. He will do as he is told. I have made that choice for him and he will not betray me. He will live. That's what it's always been about. I brought this fight and he will not die in it.

Something unexpected happens. Star growls, "Why Marshall? Why do you want her dead so badly?"

He points, "What do you think we've been hunting all these years, Star? You think the sole purpose of the fighting camps was stopping the breeder farms?"

I don't understand but she gasps, "You've been killing the children?"

His eyes harden, "And this one is no different. She cannot be left to live. None of them can."

She sounds sickened when she whispers, "You're one of the Lord's Keepers?"

He nods, "We have a job to do." He points to the sky, "He kept us safe and alive when our world turned on itself. Only he has saved us." He looks at me, "We let you live because we needed your help to stop the farms. You were making it so easy for us, bringing the little abominations right to us."

My breath is hard to get, "Where did you take them?"

He shakes his head, "We just free them. The little bit of soul they have is given back to God."

Star shouts, "Why? How could you? They were children!"

He gives us a blank look as he slowly walks behind Sarah and grabs her blonde hair, "THESE ARE CHILDREN! THOSE ARE MONSTERS MADE BY MAN! ONE MAN WHO THINKS HE'S A GOD! THERE IS ONE GOD AND HE DOES NOT ALLOW COPIES OF HIS CREATIONS!"

Sarah screams, making me twitch.

Star sounds like she might laugh at him, "So the van filled with children that we freed—those were coming to you, not the city?"

He looks at her, "Yes."

My hands twitch with a longing to hold the steel in my back. I glance around and feel a slight bit of relief at least that Leo is gone. "But you're a scientist." I point out.

He shakes his head, "I was a scientist. I have always been a man of faith. I found a perfect harmony in science, nature, and God that most wouldn't see. When the experiments with DNA started, I believed we were looking for a way to eradicate diseases, like diabetes. But that wasn't it at all. He wanted to modify what God had already perfected. If there were diseases and imperfections, they too were man-made."

Meg spits at him, "God would be ashamed of you."

He backhands her and grabs a gun from the side of the man next to him. I see him contemplate killing Meg. My insides burn until he points it at me, "You come with us."

Star grips her gun but I turn to her, "Get them out of here."

She nods. I see her brain scrambling for an idea, but this is the best one and we both know it.

Sarah is released. She cries out, running to my arms. She grips me, "Don't leave."

I drop to my knee, "I love you! No matter what happens, you remember that."

Her blue eyes are filled with tears. I have turned off my emotions though. I can't feel sad, I'm stuck in fear and hate. I pull her sweaty, little fingers from my clothes and pass her to Star. Star holds her tight.

The man with the gun to Anna's throat grins at me and tightens his finger. Meg gives me a subtle headshake. She has a plan. I give her a set look, "Go to Star."

She begs me with her face. I shake my head, "Go."

She is pushed into the dry grass, crying out from the force of it.

Marshall gives me a cruel, cold stare.

"WOLFIE!"

My head snaps around. Mary walks to us, gripping the little boy. No one holds her arm. No one has forced her to come from the side of the house. She is here freely. Of course she is.

"She has guns in her back, you idiots," she points at me. I pull a gun, firing at her face. A shot hits my left shoulder but Mary drops onto the grass, spilling the boy from her arms. He screams. Star drops to her knees, pulling Sarah and Meg to the ground.

I roll instantly, shooting the man Anna has hit in the balls. He fires at me; I feel the bullet graze my side. I pull my other gun and force my body to work against the pain. Leo comes running from behind, he has disobeyed me. He jumps Marshall from behind.

I see the gun come up. I hear a scream. I shoot a man coming from the house firing at us.

I look back for Marshall but now there are a pile of them all struggling together. Shots are being fired within the pile. I stand, running as fast as I can. I grab Leo, dragging him from the pile. Meg is on top of Marshall, holding the rifle I dropped. She fires into his chest. She runs to save Leo.

Marshall glares at me, "You'll never stop us. God wants you all dead." I see Marshall's eyes go slack as he coughs a last bit of blood.

Leo stands but his back leg buckles. He's been shot in the hind legs somewhere. He isn't the one I'm grabbing though. The dark eyes searching my face are breaking my heart. "Is he damned-well dead?" she asks and coughs.

I nod, tears are streaming my face. Star is limping, carrying Sarah. I can't see properly. Anna crawls to us. We are all covered in blood. I grip Meg to me, I can't talk. I don't know what to say.

Meg smiles, "Is Leo okay?"

I glance and him and nod, "He'll be okay. It's a leg wound."

She nods, "Good."

She has saved him. I peel back her clothes, pressing my hands into the gushing blood coming from her stomach. I know what that is—that is death. Even in the old world, a stomach shot was death.

She holds me, her eyes are wild, "The cabin is gone, Em. They burned it to the ground."

I close my eyes.

She sniffles, "They shot Ron too."

I cry harder, "I'm sorry, Meg."

She shakes her head, "At least he's waiting for me." She closes her eyes and grips me tighter, "Mary was one of them."

"I figured. I'm sorry I let her stay."

She gives me a funny smile, "I least I got to kick the crap outta her before they got there to attack." Her eyes dart at Sarah.

I laugh and cry. Sarah sobs over Meg, "Don't die, Meg."

Meg opens her dark eyes, "Hey, kid. I'm not dying, I'm going to be with Ron." Her eyes twinkle, "He owes me something." She looks at me, "God'll forgive you, Em. I'll tell him how much you done for us all when I get there." She closes her eyes again and winces, "Actually, I wouldn't be surprised if this wasn't all his plan, using you to free people. He knows you're good inside. Stop them from killing them babies, Em."

I hug her tightly, "I love you, Meg. I will."

She coughs and nods, "Me too, Em. You're as thorny as a rose bush, but like the flowers on them, you're worth the scratches." Her eyes open and she winks at Sarah, "Be good."

Sarah sobs harder, "Don't leave me, Meg."

She shakes her head, "Never."

I watch as her face goes calm. Anna is bawling with a high-pitched wheeze, holding Sarah. I can't breath and Leo has dragged himself over. He's nudging her and whining.

He smells and licks, and finally lifts his head and howls the most-haunting sound I have ever heard him make. It's like a song. He does it a few times and then bends his head. He takes a small bite of her stomach where the blood has stopped seeping. He limps away with her blood on his face, holding his leg in the air.

We lie there, helpless. I never got to ask Marshall anything. I know nothing. The sound of the little boy crying over his dead mother doesn't even touch me.

Nothing can.

My friend is dead. One of my 'us'.

Chapter Three

They arrive to the scene the way it was hours before. No one has really moved much. I'm clutching her cold-dead body to mine. Nothing can take her from me. I failed her. I let her die. I shot Mary and started it. I did this.

I didn't know I had more tears but there they were, falling from my eyes as I continued stroking her hair.

I hear the whispers and the words around me. I know Star is starting to clean everyone up. I know I should get up, but if I let her go, she's gone forever and I don't trust God enough to take her.

"Hey, Em."

I glance over to see Jake. He smiles but I can see the tears in his eyes. He takes my hand, "Come here."

I shake my head, gripping her to me, cradling her.

He pries my fingers from her, lifting me off the ground. I am about to scream and fight, when I see Will lift her so gently and carefully.

I cry harder.

Will is stone faced, but I can see it everywhere. Jake holds me to him, his body is keeping me together.

I bury my face, "I shot Mary and he shot Meg. I shouldn't have shot Mary."

I feel little fingers prying and worming their way into the

embrace. I wriggle from Jake's arms and surround the sobbing, blonde face.

Star sniffles, "She saved Leo, I saw her. Marshall put the gun up and Meg jumped. She knew what she was doing, Em."

I give Leo a dirty look and grip Sarah, "Are you hurt?"

She shakes her head and sniffles. We walk, following behind Meg's body that Will has wrapped in a sheet. Bernie has dug a hole next to a huge rose bush. Will places her in the hole. I gag a bit. He tosses a handful of dirt into the hole and steps back. Sarah and me cling to each other. I drop to my knees and watch everyone follow Will's lead.

Bernie speaks softly, "Four years ago this rose bush grew from nothing. I never planted it or watered it. It's grown from nothing and become something that makes my day a little bit better. Now I never knew Meg well, but I got the sense that she didn't come from a lot of love. I get the sense she found it in this group of people. I can't think of a better place to put someone from our little group."

Sarah smiles, still sniffling, "She was thorny like that rose bush too, just like Em."

We all laugh.

Leo finally limps over and nuzzles against me. Sarah wraps her arms around him, crying into his fur.

I see Will staring at me with a look that's filled with pain and anger.

I nod at him and feel the defeat and loss to the full

extent. I pick up my handful of dirt and get up. I stand at the edge of the hole and look down on the sheet.

I have nothing and everything to say, but I don't know how to say it. So I look up, I know she's there. I never knew anything with as much certainty as I do this. I drop the dirt from my hand and whisper, "Forgive me."

I turn and walk away. I can hear the cries and the dirt being shoveled on top of her. No... not her. She's gone. She's with Ron.

Every painful step fills me with something not good. I walk past the house and into the woods. I climb a tree and sit.

I feel safer off the ground.

My arms are bleeding and so is my side. Every branch I climb hurts me in a new way, but I can't imagine the pain she was in.

I sit in the tree and think about it all.

I feel the tree sway. Anna climbs to a branch beside me. Her face is swollen from tears and bruises. Her leg is hurt. I can see the tied bandage on it.

"I screwed up."

She nods. She knows it too.

"If I'd known they had Meg and Sarah, I would have let Will and Jake come. I would have made them come. I would have done the attack differently." I lean my face into the bark, "Shows you what I know."

She nods. She doesn't say anything. What can she say?

"Where's Andy?"

She nods at the house, "Star has him. She's getting him to bed."

I nod. I feel sick for what I've done to him. What I've taken from him. He's a small kid and I've taken the only person in the world that loved him. Mary took everything from me. I owed her, but he didn't do anything to me. Well, beyond annoy the hell outta me.

I look across the field and see Jake, Will, and Bernie stacking rocks on the mound of dirt. Sarah is standing there all alone. When the sun goes down, it makes Sarah look a bit like a ghost standing at the edge of the pile. Her blonde hair is a mess.

I force myself to watch her feel the loss of her closest friend and number-one protector. It fills me with a kind of cold hate. The kind that burns but not like fire—like too much frost and no feeling.

I want nothing like I want my revenge. Forget the world, the flashy crow, and the little kids. I want my revenge. I want to be like Leo and take a taste of her blood so I always remember.

My head starts to nod as I nearly fall asleep in the tree. I climb down, leaving Anna in the tree. She nods at me as I walk away and cross the field to the house.

Leo and Sarah are sitting at the grave. I whistle but he doesn't come.

I go inside. Bernie is restoring the power supplies and cussing about his house. He sees me and stops. Will turns and I see it.

I nod, "Just say it."

He folds his arms over his chest, "You fucking killed her."

I nod again, "I know." He walks past me and out the door. He calls Leo and Sarah inside.

Star grabs my arm and drags me to the large room off the kitchen. "We gotta stitch you up." She pulls my shirt off and sighs, "You didn't kill her."

"I left her with Mary, stupid. I came here without a clue as to what was going on, stupid. I never asked Will for help, stupid. I shot Mary and started the gun fight, stupid."

She starts to clean my shoulder and arm, "Mary was a traitorous bitch. I have never enjoyed anything, as much as I did watching you shoot her in the face; I know how awful that sounds. I feel sad that her kid was there. He's never going to be the same. At least he's sleeping now. Bernie had some old, anti-nausea medicine, I knocked him out with it." She laughs, making me laugh. We are bad people.

"We're not good with kids, Star. We need to find someone to take him."

She smiles, "I know."

I look down, "What was I thinking? I shot a woman holding her kid." I meet her eyes, "This is what's wrong with us. I can't see right from wrong in the heat of the moment. I never saw that shooting Mary would get Meg killed. I saw the shots the way they would go down, but I never imagined it would end like that."

She shrugs, "I don't see what you did was wrong. It was

a split-second decision. I see it like it was all of us or them. It's always us or them, Em." Her words burn into me, making the cold hate worse. She continues, "Meg would have been fine if she'd stayed beside me."

My lip quivers, "But Leo..."

She nods, "Yup. Meg made the same decision you made. She saw something she wanted changed and she did it. That's the world we live in. We give up our lives to save theirs, or we walk away and save ours." Her eyes tear up. She presses a needle into my wound. I tense and moan. She speaks softly again, "At least you have always been true to who you are. When I found out I was different, I never told anyone. I could have saved you at the camps and I didn't. I let them think you were the only different one."

Through clenched teeth, I mutter, "Trust me, we aren't so different. I would have lied too, if I hadn't been discovered."

Jake walks into the room. He leans against the wall, "You need to go get Leo. He's hurt and needs to come in. He and Sarah are sitting out there in the dark." His voice is cold. He turns and leaves after a second. "They're pissed."

I nod, "I would be too." She finishes and gives me some medicine, that she's sure won't do anything for me because it's expired.

I walk out into the yard, past Will and Jake. I drop to my knees when I get to the pile of stones next to the rose bush.

"We gotta go inside. It's dangerous outside."

Sarah looks at me. Her cheeks are tear-stained and her eyes so puffy they barely open, "She was my best friend."

I nod, "I know."

She runs her hand through Leo's fur, "What if that's how it is now, we just die off one by one?"

I shake my head, "I don't know." I want to lie, but the cold hate is stronger than me, and it doesn't care if she's scared.

"Meg wanted them dead. All them ones who kill the kids."

I nod, "I know."

She puts a finger out, "You have to pinky swear that you'll kill them for her. Meg always made me pinky swear." I wrap my finger around hers and she shakes it. "You kill them."

I nod, "Yes, ma'am."

She wipes her little face and nods, "Okay, me and Leo will come in." She stands, and sure enough, he stands and follows her inside. I look at the grave, "Night, Meg." My eyes lift to the stars. I imagine she is one of them. Anyone who would do something so brave as to save Leo with their life, is hero enough for a place in the sky.

I stand and walk behind them to the house. Will wraps an arm around Sarah and carries her upstairs. I slap my leg at Leo. He tries to follow Sarah but I snap my fingers. He bows his head and walks with me to the kitchen. He's still limping and holding that leg in the air.

We get to the room. I pat the table, "Can you jump up?" I know he's got to be at least as much as I weigh. There is no way I'll get him on the table.

Jake walks in, "You need some help?"

I nod. Leo bares his teeth instantly. Jake gives him a look, "I need to put you on this table and you can bite me if you want to, but you're going up there."

Leo snarls but Jake ignores it. He reaches around and grabs him. He places him on the table, getting nips and snorts from the huge timber wolf. I see a bit of blood on Jake's arm. He doesn't even flinch.

Leo lies down on the table, looking uneasy. Star puts her hands up, "This you can handle. I'm not getting bit."

I stroke his face, "Hey, it's me and you now." He yawns and I nod, "Settle in." I grab some scissors and cut back the tufts of fur. The bullet made a perfect hole through his leg. It missed the bone completely. I look at Jake, "Wanna pet him?"

He laughs, "Yeah sure. He's already done his worst."

I start the cleaning and look at Jake, "I'm sorry."

He shrugs, "You aren't ever going to trust me or Will. I get why you don't trust him, but me, I have never done anything but be your friend."

I nod, "I know and I'm sorry. I wish I'd asked for help. I had no idea what we were walking into."

He nods, "There used to be a saying, Dad always said it when me and Will were fighting. There is no 'I' in team. You either work as a team to win, or you lose as a group of individuals."

I sew the wound together. Leo sits, letting Jake pet his

face. He doesn't bite him. He's as content as he can be. He trusts me again.

Will walks in, "Sarah is sleeping."

I look up at him, "Thanks."

He turns and walks out. Jake makes a face, "He might kill you in your sleep."

I snort, "God, I hope so." And I do. Because if he doesn't, the cold hate is going to consume me and I'll kill everyone until I've satisfied it.

I understand why I never let anything in beyond Leo. Things and people end. They don't take everything with them though; there is always a little bit left over that burns you inside.

We finish with Leo and force medicine down his throat. Jake helps him down, getting bit again. We follow Jake to the living room and slump into the huge chairs. The house is quiet. Anna and Bernie are snuggled into a chair. Star is sitting on the floor next to the TV that doesn't serve a purpose anymore. Will is on the couch. Jake sits beside him. I sit on the floor and let Leo come rest his head on my lap. Bernie gets up and passes us some of whatever they're all drinking. I sniff it, smelling things that make my body shudder.

I take a big drink and feel the burn. It feels good, warming me against the cold hate.

I look at the glass and wonder who is going to talk first.

No one does for a long time, but then Jake smiles, "I want to toast to Meg. The first girl who ever told me that I was what she called 'a long sip of ice-cold water on a hot day'. I asked her when she'd ever had ice-cold water and she replied, never. I just heard Momma say it whenever we saw something as yummy as you roaming the woods. To Meg."

We all laughed and drank a huge gulp. My head started to spin.

Star held up her glass, "To Meg, thank you for showing me how to cook deer properly, since I couldn't do it, even if the damned deer got up and told me how."

I laughed harder and took back another big gulp.

Anna whispered into Bernie's ear. He held up his glass, "This is from Anna. To Meg, the girl who told me to tell Emma to stick it up her kazoo, when I told her she wouldn't let me and Bernie date."

I laughed and nodded. Kazoo was a weird word I swore she made up. I imagined she made up most of what she said.

I held up my glass, "To Meg, my sister. Thank you for showing me how to not take things so seriously." I drank it back, knowing it wasn't funny but it was true. She was always chewing a piece of grass and telling me to mind my business about Bernie and Anna. She was always telling me to just love both brothers and let them sort out the details. I drank back the last of my drink.

"How did you meet her?" Bernie asked.

I sniffled, "She saved my life. She saved me from something bad."

Bernie looks surprised, "She saved you?"

I nod, "We were with the others, in cages. I was about to be... next thing I knew, he was dead and there was little Meg cussing at me to hurry up and run away. She'd stabbed him in the side of his eye with a nail. She was a savage. She didn't stop talking for days. Momma this, and momma that, and Auntie Heather, and Leo was sort of useless for a pet. He wasn't as great as her precious hounds." My eyes gloss over and I finish the drink, "She was one of my first friends, like a little sister." I glance at Anna. She smiles and winks at me.

Bernie smiles, "She was a genuinely-good person."

Jake laughs, "She was just crazy enough to be fun, but had more sense in one finger than anyone I've ever met."

I laugh and hold my glass out with the last drink of the liquid, "To Meg."

I wake the next morning stiff, achy, and hateful. My whole body is an angry mess. I climb from the bed filled with a snuggly eleven-year old and walk to the bathroom. I pull off my clothes and look at myself naked. I'm a mess. Bruises, cuts, stitches, and dried blood.

I sigh and climb into the shower. The hot water is amazing. The soap stings everywhere, but every time I think about the pain, my brain chimes in and thinks, aren't you lucky to be alive and feeling that pain. The cold hate feels lessened by the people in the house.

I climb out to find Sarah sitting in a corner in the bathroom. I wrap myself with a towel and walk to her. I drop to my knees, "You okay?"

She shakes her head, "I had a bad dream and then I woke up, and Andy was screaming and crying again."

I hold my hand out to her, "Come on. I think I saw some of those packets of that sauce cook used to make you. I'll see if Bernie can whip you up some home fries and that sauce. Maybe breakfast will help Andy too. Bernie had potatoes last time I was here."

She perks up and stands. I pull on clean clothes of Star's and we go downstairs to try to start our day.

We find only Jake in the kitchen, eating a bar. He smiles at me, "You look pretty."

I laugh and nod, "You seen Bernie?"

His eyes darken, "He's in bed still." I realize what that means and grimace, "Oh."

He gives me a look, "Trust me, he didn't have much choice on the matter. He tried to be a gentleman last night after you went to bed."

I put a hand up, "I don't need to know."

He laughs, "Haven't you ever heard that misery loves company?"

I smile, "I heard that before."

Sarah smiles brightly, "Me too."

He smirks, "It's true."

I nod toward Sarah, "You want to help me make some breakfast?"

He smiles, "What are we having?"

Chapter Four

Bernie puts gold tacks on the places he knows for sure have camps or towns. It dawns on me, I don't know anything about the world we live in.

"I didn't know there were so many."

He looks up, "There are a lot of survivors, especially in the Midwest. The East Coast was completely destroyed in the tidal waves and hurricanes, but the winters were what got most of the people. The disease was worse there too, with the dense population and all."

He places a red felt dot on the towns he knows have Lord's Keepers. "Here and here are the worst I've heard of. This place has some but it's a mix of traders and Keepers."

I look down, "I've seen them lots, always trying to get kids to come with them. I figured they were either perverts or just trying to help the children with no parents."

He nods, "I'm sure it's a special mixture."

I snort and cross my arms, "How will we get to them all?"

Will nods, "Same as we did with the breeder farms."

I give him a look, "You haven't been to the towns much, have you?"

He furrows his dark brow, "Not a ton, why?"

I shrug, "There aren't a lot of medical types who don't know how to shoot a gun properly. Those people are survivors. They're more like me and you."

His stare gets cold, "Then we should fit in famously."

Bernie looks like he's thinking, "The thing you're forgetting though, the townspeople want you to succeed. There's talk of you and the rebellion."

I frown, “The flashy crow isn’t going to get us anywhere with those people. Yeah, the ones who had family at the farms sure, but we’d have to free the work farms before any of them would really care. Women aren’t as important as men, not any more.”

Bernie laughs, “Not since we went back to constantly barbecuing in a cave.”

I frown again but Will laughs. Anna gives me a confused look as she leaves the room. Star points at a spot in the middle, “There is a work camp right near there. I bet the majority of that town has family in the camps.”

Bernie nods, still chuckling, “Right, we went there once. I remember that. When do we leave?”

I looked around, “We… is a bad move. We includes Sarah, Anna who can't talk, and Jake who is Jake. Bernie, no offense, but you aren’t exactly badass either.”

He puts a hand in the air, “I’m good with staying. I don’t care what happens out there, never have.”

Star nods, “So me, you, and Will?”

I nod, “And Andy. We need to find him some people to take care of him. We could work that woman-slaver angle if we have to. I’ve seen that.” I wish I hadn’t.

Jake shakes his head, “I’m coming. Leo still isn’t a hundred percent; he’s staying and Anna is never going to let you leave her here.”

Anna walks back in with a drink. I don’t meet her gaze, “I’m sure Bernie can take that.”

Bernie gives me a confused look, “You think so?”

I nod, “You underestimate the effect love has on people.”

He shakes his head, “I think you underestimate my role in our love.” I laugh but Anna grabs my arm, ignoring when I wince from the wound on it.

I shake my head and just say what I'm thinking, "You can't come. Just stop being crazy and think. This house is our best bet at survival in the winter. When it comes, we won't have the cabin. Think about your last winter? Think about the fact you and Jake hid outside my cabin, stealing water and nearly dying. It was spring then. And Bernie can't keep this place safe, now that people know where it is. We don't know if any of Marshall's people made it out of here. We need Sarah, Bernie, and Leo to stay safe. Leo is hurt. He can't come with me. We need this house to stay safe. You're the only one."

Her eyes burn. She whispers, "Damn you."

I nod, "I know if anyone can keep Leo and Sarah safe, it's you."

She makes her wheeze and storms from the room.

Bernie gives me a look, "Wow, you came up with that faster than I would have."

I nod, "It's true and it's the only way she's gonna stay. I could see you weren't going to say anything anyway."

His eyes soften, "Thank you." He knows we're going to die, more than likely and doesn't want her to come. We're always more than likely going to die. The fact only Meg is gone is some kind of miracle.

Will gives me a look, "When do you want to leave?"

"Now."

Star looks annoyed, "Really?"

I nod, "I want this over. I want to be back before the people from the camp have time to get here, if any did get away."

Jake watches me from the corner, "I'm coming." He turns and leaves. I look at Will who clenches his jaw, "He's not going to back down."

I shrug, "I'll break his legs, he'll stay."

I storm after him. He looks back and me and grins, taking off running. I can still see the way he favors his leg that was hurt.

I chase him up the stairs. “You aren’t coming.”

He gives me a smirk, “You going to stop me?”

I nod, “I am.”

“You aren’t the boss, flashy crow. You may have everyone else convinced you’re the boss, but I don’t buy it. I watched you for months. You were lonely. You were scared. I saw it. You read those books in the window of that cabin and your face softened, in a way I only see when you’re with me.” He points, “You can deny it all you want, but I know you better than anyone. I know you better than you know yourself.” He closes the door, leaving me standing in the hallway with my heart beating a mile a minute.

I never thought about the fact he watched me.

I turn and walk into our room. Sarah is napping with Andy on the bed. I lie down beside her, stroking her soft, blonde hair. She opens her eyes slowly, “Mom?” She sees me and blushes, “Hey, Em.”

I smile, “Missing your mom?”

She shakes her head, “No.”

I smile wider, “It's okay if you are. I miss my family all the time."

She shakes her head, "Just missing Meg. The rest of my family is here."

I don’t want to say it, but I need to be honest with her, "I have to go, kid. I gotta stop those people hurting the kids for Meg. Then I have to deal with my dad.”

Her happy look is gone, “Take me with you. Don’t leave me alone.”

I grab her and hold her tight, “Anna is going to stay and Leo and Bernie. If I could get Jake to stay, I would but he’s being an ass.”

She shakes and snuggles into me more, “Don’t leave, Em. We’re safe here.”

I nod, "But those people that were going to hurt me, they're hurting the little kids all the time now. We have to go save those kids. Remember, Meg wanted them all dead."

She looks at me with her glossy, blue eyes, "Okay. Meg wanted them kids saved. She said that God loves all kids, no matter how they came to be here. She said them men was the devil and not servants of God at all."

I smiled, "No one knew God like Meg did."

Sarah's eyes glance around the room, "Uh, Em, just don't bring them here." She glances at Andy, "One bratty kid is enough."

I laugh softly, "I'm taking that one with me."

She shakes her head, "He isn't so bad with Mary not being here to coddle him over everything. He wasn't even hers."

I don't understand, "What?"

She nods, "When Marshall got to the cabin, he kept saying that she was lucky he found that brat for her, and she should be grateful he spared the soul of her baby."

I wince, "Oh God."

She nods and I wonder if she understands it all. I look at Andy, "So he isn't like me?"

She shakes her head, "No. Meg said that's why they let him live, like us. They was going to let us live too, 'cause we're normal." Her words burn me, she doesn't know it, but they do. I don't say anything. I kiss her forehead and take a deep breath of her before I get up, "You help Anna with that kid then. If you want him to stay, you gotta do the work."

She smiles, "I don't like him that much, but I don't hate him. Not the way I hated Mary. Meg said all he needed was a spanking."

I laughed, "Well, don't go overboard on those either. Beating someone rarely changes who they are, and only really makes you feel better for a short amount of time." I learned that in a book of my dad's. It was about parenting, single parenting.

I wave, "I'll see you when I get back. Stay in the house with them, don't stray, and take Leo everywhere with you."

She nods, "Be safe."

I grin and leave the room. I hunt the house for Leo. I find him camped out. It's his way of healing. He always hides under something. Old wolf instincts.

I crawl under the huge coffee table and curl into him. The smell of his fur makes my heart ache. I stroke him. He makes his wolf sound and licks my hand. I grab his huge face and make him look into my eyes, "You keep them safe. You stay safe. No coming after me, no matter what. I'll come for you, I swear it. Even if I have to drag myself here from wherever I am, I'll make it back, but you stay. You hear me?"

His eyes study my face. He licks my cheek. I lean into his face, "I love you too."

"Keep Anna and Sarah safe the most. If Bernie or Andy have to be risked to save them, I want you to do it."

I don't know if he understands me but I know how his loyalty works. And how he feels about Andy. Damned kid.

I crawl back out and kiss him. I point, "You stay with Anna and Sarah."

He yawns. He knows he's sick. His wound hadn't got infected yet but it's still sore.

I leave the house and walk to the garage. Bernie is passing Will bags that look like the military compound bags.

"How did you get all this shit?"

He grins at me, "I may or may not have stolen it."

Anna glares at me from the house. Jake nudges me as he walks out, eating moose jerky, "You think she's mad now—wait till she finds out Andy is staying."

I glare at him.

He smiles wide, “You better be nice to me, or I’ll tell her.”

I shove him. Will scowls, “Stop screwing around and load the van.” He nods at the back, “Put some gas in, Jake. Be useful for once.”

Jake flips him the bird but gets the gas jugs.

I shake my head.

We finish loading and climb into the van. Anna doesn’t budge. Bernie gives me a hug.

Star gives me a devious smile, “I see we’re missing a passenger.”

I nod, “Sarah wants him to stay.”

She frowns, “Well, at least we don’t have to listen to him.”

Bernie looks confused, “You aren’t leaving that kid here?”

I nod, “We are.” I close the door, shouting at him, “Take care of my family, Bernie.”

He nods at me through the window. We drive away and I see the desperate anger on Anna’s face. I hate it. Sarah waves through the upstairs window. I scramble over Jake and Will, not thinking and climb over Will’s body to hang mine out the window, waving my arm. Her face lights up.

“Em, I’m not complaining, but I can’t see.”

I climb off him and sit back against the metal wall. Star gives me a funny look, “Sometimes you do the weirdest things. Like caring for that kid. What do you care if she sees you waving?”

I frown, “I don’t want her last memory of me to be that she waved and I didn’t wave back. I know how that feels.”

I look down at my boots. I’m tired in a way I’ve never been. It’s like it’s in my soul. My body can heal from anything, but I’m seeing that my heart can’t. Meg’s death is a sore that won’t heal over, not properly, and Leo being hurt and not with me, is an awful feeling. My mind is playing horrid tricks on me, suggesting things like Leo could get an infection, and die thinking I abandoned him in a house with other people.

I wrap my arms around myself and try not to think about any of it. Marshall is dead, and maybe he did kill Meg, but she killed him right back. She saved all of us. She saved me. I think Leo is the thing that saved the good parts in me, the parts that Granny made, and I think his death would have killed those parts off. Then I would be a shell of a human, like Will. That makes me shudder.

"You cold?"

I glance up at Star and shake my head.

She gives me a faint smile, "You know, you aren't what I expected you to be."

I nod, "Same goes for you. I thought you were weak, giggly, and annoying."

Her eyebrow lifts, "So what you're saying is, you don't feel like I'm like that?"

I nod, "I think you're more than that."

She looks wounded, "But you're not saying, I'm not like that."

I laugh, "No. You turn it on too well to not have at least a little of that in you."

She smiles, "A girl's gotta do… ya know?"

I shake my head. I don't know. She must have read it in a book somewhere. It sounds like one of those lines.

Jake climbs into the back with us and sits on the floor of the van next to me.

"We could have just stayed at the house, Em. We could say fuck it, let your dad ruin the world, and let the religious psychos kill those bratty kids. We could stay at the house and make it work.

I sigh, "Until when? Until they come and kill us, or take Sarah and put her in a breeder farm, or those kids take over the world, or the religious nuts come for me again?"

He shrugs, "We coulda stayed."

I lean my head back and close my eyes, "I need to stop my dad."

Jake grunts and stretches his long legs out and balls a jacket on the floor. He lays down on it, turning his back on me. The feeling of him next to me is like Leo being there. My boot is touching his leg, like I always do with Leo. If I sleep without him, I turn sideways in the night, searching the bed for him in my sleep.

The ride makes me sleepy. I close my eyes, exhausted and worn out.

I wake to screaming, jolted and disjointed. It's my own.

Star gives me a confused look, “You okay? You just started screaming.”

I shake my head, “I don’t know.” I climb over Jake’s massive body and slip into the front seat. I pull my knees into my chest and look out the window.

“Unroll it.”

I look at Will. He smiles at me, “Unroll the window.”

A faint trickle of a grin crosses my lips. I press the button I vaguely recall, and lower the window. Instantly, warm wind bursts in. I hang my hand out, feeling like a kid again. Star laughs at something Jake says. I glance back at the tired look on his face as he rubs his eyes and mumbles, “If we had music, I could almost believe the world didn’t end. Feels like summer out there.”

I smile when he reaches up between the seats and fumbles with the stereo. A shiny disk comes sliding out. I don’t even recall them, except maybe as movie disks.

He nods, “Ohhhh yeah.” He pushes it back into the slot and presses buttons.

Will gives him a look, “What are you doing?”

He gives a cheesy grin as a song starts. It sounds crazy, my ears hurt instantly. A girl starts singing.

Jake starts dancing. Star gives him a weird look but then her eyes light up as the chorus starts. “BIG IN JAPAN! AHHHHH!” she screams and starts knee dancing with him. I’m partially horrified but fascinated too. They look crazy, but it looks too fun.

Will sings along, like he heard it yesterday. He gives me a look, “What, I loved Dragonette.”

I see it for a second, the glimpse of the person he might have been once. He dances in the seat and turns up the music. I’m uncomfortable with them dancing and singing, like I should too but I don’t want to. I lean my upper body out the window, and I see how it could have been. With my eyes closed it’s so easy. We’re young and fun, and the wind is warm. The beat starts to find its way into my body too. The wind on my face and the hot smell of summer makes everything romantic; it lasts almost as long as the song, but a terrible pain mixes with a sound from the real world. The real one I live in is brought back, as I pull myself in and notice the crimson trickle on my forearm. I’m about to say something to Will when he slams on the brakes. I am thrown forward, but his hand is across my chest, holding me back. I grunt as the van stops.

Men are on the road in front of us with guns, they’re atop horses.

“Is it the others?” I ask.

He shakes his head, “Far worse. Don’t fight. I’ll see if I can negotiate with them.”

I start to shake my head, “Will…”

He takes my hand, “I won't let them hurt you.”

Star and Jake are both rubbing sore spots as a man walks up to my door. He points his rifle at my open window, “Get out.” He’s close to Will’s age. He looks disheveled but not dirty or hungry. He has shaggy, blonde hair and a steely look in his eyes. He’s a hardened man.

I swallow, opening the door slowly.

“Don’t,” Will mutters, as I’m about to hit the man with the door. I take a deep breath and let him grab me by the bloody spot on my arm.

He gives me a charming grin, “Sorry, I was aiming for the tires.” He is handsome with straight, white teeth. He winks at me. I want to claw his eyes out. Instead, I let him drag me back, placing the barrel against my head, “Get out or I won't accidentally miss again.” Will meets my eyes with desperation. “It’s okay.”

I shake my head. The man whispers in my ear, “Whoa, girl. Stay calm and I’ll be gentle, I swear it.”

My brow knits together. Will shakes his head slowly, “Look at me, baby.” He climbs out as one man opens the back door. He hauls Star out violently, holding her next to his body. She is shaking with rage. I see it on the men’s faces when they look at Star. Fury fills me. One of the men rides over, lifting her up onto his horse.

The man who had been holding Star, butts Will in the stomach with his gun. Will doubles over. They wrap a rope around him and Jake. There are at least a dozen men. The man with his greasy fingers on me, pulls me backwards. He climbs on a horse, “Get on.”

I am about to fight but a man hits Jake in the back of the legs, dropping him to his knees. I climb on the back of the horse. “Don’t hurt them.”

He nods, “Put them in the van.”

I haven’t ridden a horse since I was a tiny kid. My friend Rebecca had them. He grabs my arms and wraps them around his chest, “Hold tight and no funny business or you can sit up front, and God knows where my hands will sit.”

I nod. My breathing is hitching in my throat. Jake and Will are shoved back in the van. A few men get in with them. Will’s face is the last thing I see as the door closes. Blackness envelops me as something is stuffed over my head. I breathe heavily, against the stale feel of the material. I don’t have a plan but something dark fills me when I hear Star start to protest.

My worst nightmare is about to come true, the sound of my own ripping and tearing. Only it's worse, my only sister will also join me as I'm victimized. Silent tears stream my cheeks. I've never felt fear like this. Not even at the farms.

We ride for a long time. I hold myself to him, smelling him and the horse and rocking against him in the heat. It's intense. I try to stay in the mountains for the summer months. It's brutal down in the lower lands. The thing over my head makes breathing almost impossible. My eyes close against my wishes. I feel myself melting into his back. He chuckles and stops the horse. He pulls the black thing off my head.

I can't open my eyes. My breaths are shallow. I feel his fingers on my lips. It sparks an old reaction. My head shoots up. I open my eyes. We're in the middle of the forest.

He smiles, "What's your name?"

My hands twitch with the want to choke and kill him, but they won't move beyond that.

He lifts my face, resting a spout against my lower lip. He winks his sparkly steel-colored eyes at me, "Drink up."

The warm water pours into me. I gulp it back, feeling panic and despair starting to stir inside of me.

He pulls it away and dumps some over my head. He rubs it into my hair. I shake my head, lifting my weak hands over my face.

"Sorry about the hood."

I shake my head, wiping my face clean. He gives me an odd look, "Why do I get the feeling you're plotting my death right now, behind those pretty eyes?"

I nod, "I am."

He smiles, "I bet you could kill me too couldn't you?"

"Yup."

He laughs, casually, "I might have to keep you all to myself."

He turns and boots the horse lightly. We don't stand a chance at catching up to the rest of them. The water refreshes me. I see Star's body draping over the horse. She passed out from the hood.

I take a deep breath, fighting the butterflies in my belly and grab his throat. I try to wrap my arm around his neck as I wrap my legs around his waist. He jumps off the horse, rolling us both. We land with me on top of him. I choke him. He hits my arms, knocking them back. I swing, punching him in the mouth. He laughs and rolls us. He is on top of me but I'm squeezing his middle, choking him that way. He makes a noise, as he sits up and smacks me. I cry out, squeezing harder. His fingers curl around my throat. They're huge. I know he could snap my neck.

He smiles a bloody grin, "Stalemate."

I don't know what that means. I feel his grip loosen, letting my legs relax. He presses his bloody lips on mine. I gag and cry out as he kisses me. He stands up, grabs my arms and drags me to the horse.

"Now you get to sit up front. You pain in the ass." He hauls me up onto the horse. His hands slide around my middle to the reins, "Mess with me and I won't keep you safe."

My jaw trembles. I can taste his blood in my mouth.

My head is slumped as we ride up the hill fast, after everyone else. I need Leo. I need Anna. I wish I'd waited.

We crest the hill and turn into the bushes where the van is parked on the dirt road. I can barely make out a goat path of sorts. My butt and body are aching. I need more water. We get into a camp consisting of cabins like mine. There are a dozen of them though.

I see Will and Jake kneeling on the ground. Will's eyes meet mine. He's searching me for signs of bad things. I shake my head subtly. Jake glances at me. He looks terrified. I know I am too.

Star gets dragged to a group of men. Her legs are jelly. They toss a big bucket of water on her. She screams.

A man walks over to Jake, kicking him in the stomach. He gags and falls forward. The man takes a long drink from his whiskey bottle and backhands Will. He spits the whiskey all over both of them. Just as that happens, Star screams again. A man is mauling her.

I wince and elbow the man holding me by the throat and jump off my horse. I run to tackle the man grabbing at Star's arms, but something happens and I'm pulled back with my hands tied at my sides. I thump on my back on the hard ground. The wind gets knocked out of me.

The man laughs. Will and Jake look ready to attack.

"Good to see I haven't lost it!" The man on the horse gets down and lifts me off the ground to my knees.

One of the men near Star nods at me, "You have a bit of trouble with that one, Fish?"

I growl as he kneels next to me, "This one is mine. She's a wild cat." He lifts me up, keeping the rope around my arms tight.

The guy carrying me looks at Will, "You lads don't mind sharing your lady friends, then we'll be happy to let you stay. Always looking for more recruits to help out."

Will nods, "Yeah, whatever man. We picked them up along the way. Not so friendly though."

Jake gives him a look but nods along with him, "That one is mean." His eyes land on me.

I snarl at him.

"Name's Fischer, everyone calls me Fish."

Will nods, "I'm Will, this is my brother Jake."

"Well, we need to make sure y'all are alright with this arrangement before we untie you, I'm sure you understand."

Will shrugs, "Whatever. We thought you were the others. I'm pleasantly surprised."

I spit at him. I assume we're putting on an act.

Fish grabs my face in his hands, "That wasn't nice. You just spit on my new friend." I wince as his hand comes back, landing in the same spot as the last one.

"Say sorry to my friend. He was nice enough to pick you two up and save you from the others and this is how you show gratitude?"

I press my lips together. He lets me go and backhands me. I fall back over, unable to stop myself.

"You're right boys, this one needs some manners." He bends to pick me up but I manage to kick him in the balls, hard. I slide my leg behind his left leg, dropping him to the ground. I get to my knees, pulling the rope free. I jump up, running across the small fire area and tackle the man dragging my sister to a cabin. The force of the tackle takes him right into a huge bush. He screams as my fists start making their first contact. Someone grabs at me but I flip him over too. Something hits my back but my rage has taken ahold.

Only the gunshot stops me.

"What in sam hell is going on here?" A fist smokes my cheek as I turn my head, recognizing the voice. "Emma?"

I'm knocked into the bush on my back. I swear the world is spinning and Jack's face is in the middle.

"You know this bitch?"

I shake my head, slightly dazed, "Hey, Jack."

He chuckles, "Easy there, Fish. This is the girl who has been starting the revolution to bring down the slave camps."

I sit up, seeing the savage face of Fish. I wipe the blood from the corner of my mouth. Jack points, "Will, Jake? What the hell is going on here?"

I shove the guy next to me and stand up.

Fish gets right in my face, "This is the girl you sent word about?"

I snarl, leaning into his face. His hand roaming the front of my body is still fresh in my mind. Star shoves the man holding her arm. She stands next to me and smirks, “How are your balls, Fish?" There is craziness in her eyes.

He glares at me, “Somebody is gonna be sorry.” He points at me, “We ain’t done here.”

I nod, “I agree.”

He smirks, “Oh me and you are gonna wrestle some more.”

I sneer, “Name the place and time. I’ll be there with bells on.” I read it in a book. I love that line. I don’t get the point of wearing bells though. Sounds silly. You'd never sneak through the woods here with bells on.

He laughs at it though. He takes the whiskey from the guy who spat on Will and Jake.

Jack takes the bottle, “I think there has been more than enough of this going on. Now, I don’t even want to know what’s been going on. This is Emma, Star, Will and Jake. They were kind enough to let me stay at their camp and never abused me. They will find the same thing here, or I will let this one kick the ever-loving shit outta ya. You ain’t even seen her in action. Give her a bow or a gun and damn.” They eyeball me up, but I'm ready to go. My fury is boiling through my veins. Jack points at Will, “Y’all owe my friends some apologies.”

Star leaps into Jack’s arms. She kisses his cheek, “Thank you. Thank you.” I can see her shaking, it bugs me bad. I know what was about to happen. We are surrounded by the kind of men who tear clothes and think the world owes them everything. There is something in Jack's eyes, beyond surprise to see us. He might be scared for us.

Tears are streaming Star's cheeks. Jack gives a deadly glare to the men and then smiles softly at Star as he wraps an arm around her shoulder, “Come get cleaned up.” I can see her holding her shirt in place, where the rip was. I’m angry in a way I don't like getting.

Fish unties Will and Jake and puts a hand out, “Sorry about that.”

Will’s face clenches. Jake takes the hand, “It’s cool. We probably would have done the same, maybe not raped your friends though. That’s kinda sad, you all need to force women to sleep with you.”

Will laughs as Jake winks at them. But then he does something I'm not expecting. Jake walks up to the guy who spat on them and punches him in the face, hard. Instantly, he winces and holds his hand, “Ow, goddamn.” He points at the swaying man, who drops to a knee, “I hate being spit on.” He looks back at me, “Wanna get cleaned up?”

I eyeball Fish and then turn to Jake, “Yup.”

Fish smiles at me, “Me and you baby, me and you. This is happening.”

Will steps in front of him, I can see his threshold is about to snap. I step between them, turning my back on Fish. I look up into Will’s face, “Don't.”

He looks at me, not changing his stance. He's about to say something to me, but instead, he leans over me, into Fish, “I’m going to gut you like a real fish if you even look at her.”

Jake leans in too, “That goes double for me.”

I feel Fish step back, “Oh shit. I didn’t realize I was stepping into a threesome.”

My cheeks burn. I step past Will and walk to one of the cabins, after I grab a bucket of water from the stack of them near the fire pit. I drag it to a cabin and close the door. I sit in the corner of the cabin with the bucket next to me, and cry. I release, like I haven’t done in forever. I need the softness of those paws to wrap around me and make me feel better.

Instead, I get warm hands pulling me into his lap. I didn’t even hear the cabin door.

“You scared me.”

I just cry, I don’t care that he sees me cry again and feels my weakness. I need to let go of the rage and savage anger. I don't have it in me to let go without murdering someone, so being held is a good alternative.

A knock on the cabin door stops the tears. I look up into Will's face. I had expected Jake to come, in but I wanted it to be Will. His eyes are hard and mean but I know it's not for me.

He makes a face like he wants to say something he can't. "You know I'm going to have a very hard time not killing all of them."

I sniffled and wiped my face, "Me too. I don't even get what they are."

His eyes are dark, "Raiders. They're thieves. I've heard of the groups of men who ride horses like old bandits from the movies and steal. I just didn't know Jack was one of them."

The knock happens again. He sighs, "Come in."

Jack walks in with a severe look on his face, "Look, y'all can stay the night, but after that, you gotta go. These are not good people. I stay with them for the winters, always have. They used to be different. Too many winters here in the hills. We used to have fun robbing the people who had things, but they started getting worse and worse."

I frown, "Jack, you gotta come with us."

He shakes his head, "They'll be plotting against you. I need to stay and get them drunk off their asses, so you can get away. I scouted out the rebel camps because I needed somewhere else to go for the winters. I can't stay with them anymore. They've taken this all too far."

Will nods, "That house I told you about—that's where we will be for the winter. You need to meet us there."

Jack's eyes harden, "I doubt I'll get out of here in time. You know summer is only a couple months and then it's snow in these hills. I don't want them tracking you. I'll be staying behind. Next spring though, I'll see if I can't get away."

I swallow hard, shaking my head, "No, Jack. When I was little, my Granny told me that when a bear gets the taste for man flesh he has to be put down. Your boys here, they ain't any different than the others. They can't be allowed to live. They're like a pack of strays, hunting together and getting more and more savage. They toyed with us."

He looks like he might argue but he nods, "Y'all leave me to it then. I'll make sure."

I'm about to shake my head, but I can see his decision is made. He isn't going to hurt them or make them stop what they're doing. He's going to make sure they stay up the hill drunk, but he can't kill them. They're his 'us' like Will, Jake, Anna, \ Leo, and Sarah are mine. Damn—and Star. They mean more to him than he's letting on.

But I can do something about them. They mean nothing to me. I can do a lot of things to a pack of men who make the tearing sound.

I smile politely, "Okay then. We will leave tomorrow and stay in one cabin tonight."

He nods, "I'll get Jake and Star in here too." He turns and leaves. Will looks at me and whispers, "You can't. Whatever you are planning—stop."

I nod, "Maybe."

Jake and Star come in the cabin as I stand and wipe my face clean. I scrub my body, getting faster and more feverish with my scrubbing. I know what I'm removing. It makes me shudder to know how it could have gone.

Star has clearly done the same thing. Her face and arms are red from scrubbing.

Jake is clean too. I smirk, "That was some punch you threw."

He snorts, "I think I need lessons."

Will shakes his head, "You need way more than that."

He scowls at his brother, "At least I can have a conversation with someone, without making them want to kill me."

I laugh and nod, "He has a point there."

Will gives us both a narrowed gaze.

I glance at Star, "How comfortable are you with killing them all?"

She nods, "Very."

I bite my lips, "We need guns. I'll go see if I can get some."

Will shakes his head, "You stay here, for Christ's sake. You go out there and they'll all start thinking about the fact you're a girl and they're not." He sighs and runs his hands through his dirty, whisky-soaked hair, "I'll go."

He doesn't look at us as he leaves the cabin. I wait a couple seconds and glance at Jake, "I'm going out the back window, I'll be back in a minute. Make it seem like I'm laying down, in case he gets back before me."

Jake opens his mouth to argue but I leave. Sneaking out the window isn't so hard. I've done it hundreds of times, but the camp is bustling. I creep along the back, seeing a man sharpening a knife on a log. He must be a guard of sorts. I walk up behind him, staying low to the bushes. I sit next to him on the log, making sure no one sees us. He jumps a little, flashing an angry glare at me. He's not much older than me but tired looking. His dark hair is messy and longer.

"What the hell do you want?" he grumbles.

I notice the bit of dried blood on his sleeve. I don't recall him from the fighting, but I'm sure I nearly killed him. "How do you know Jack?"

He looks at me like he might snap but his eyes are scary like mine. He looks deeply into mine and something he sees in there kills off his anger. "He's my dad."

My stomach falls as I nod slowly. I need to see him as one of them bad ones. "Do y'all rape a lot of women?"

He gives me a shocked look but then sighs and shakes his head, "I've never done anything like that before. I didn't even know what Fish was doing. If Dad had been here that wouldn't have happened but he's been off lately. Taking a lot of trips."

I think for a second, "Who is Fish?"

"Dad and him have been friends for a while. We found this old camp and have spent a few winters here. We have been safe and sound and not worrying about much."

I nod, "I think Jack was looking for somewhere for you and him to go to."

He shakes his head, "He's always gone lately, and Fish and them don't seem as bad when he's around."

I whisper, "Do you want out?"

He glances down and gives a single, subtle nod. I get up and leave. I'm not making him any promises, but I like Jack and this guy is the reason Jack won't let us kill them. He didn't want me to know his son was in on the assaults.

I sneak behind the buildings to the cabin they had tried dragging Star into. I hear men arguing. It freezes me up inside. I don't budge. I hold my breath and wait.

I can't hear what they're saying, but I can hear Jack. I can only assume it's Fish but then I hear Will. I creep to the scum-covered window with the huge bush in front of it.

I can hear their voices better.

"She isn't going to go for that. She's all or nothing," Will says.

"The rest were never like this. Fish has lost it. He's got them doing things—bad things." Jack says in a hushed tone.

I lean against the house and realize they want to only kill the ones they have to.

I bite my lips. Can I walk away, knowing they would have hurt me and Star?

A branch snaps behind me. I spin just in time to see a fist coming for my face. I duck and tackle. Taking Fish to the ground. He grabs at my arms, laughing and rolling us so he's on top of me. I scratch and pinch and fight, but he pins me.

He is breathing heavily and looking down on me with a huge grin, "You are a savage."

I clench my jaw, looking for my out or his weakness.

He smiles, "Come on, Emma. You want me. I can sense it. You like it rough. I can tell this sort of thing about girls and you are just my type."

I snarl, "You're not my type, Fish. I like to be on top." I roll us as I wrap my thighs around his waist. I squeeze hard into his kidneys. He screams and it's my turn to laugh. He wraps his massive hands around my throat but I punch his windpipe hard. He chokes and I roll us again. I pin him to the ground, pressing on his throat and digging my fingernails around his Adam's apple.

He laughs in a wheeze. He doesn't have the dead look in his eyes, he's enjoying the wrestling. Gasping for air and confused, I shake my head, "What are we doing? Why do you want this? Is this fun for you? Are you insane?"

He grabs a fist full of my hair, dragging it down to his face, "Women are dead inside. It's rare to see one so alive." He smells my greasy, dirty hair. He closes his eyes, "I just wanted to know what you would feel like in my arms." In the closed slits of his eyes, I see tears forming that are about to fall down his cheeks. I don't know what is happening.

My arm is grabbed as someone shouts, "WHAT THE HELL?" I flinch but it's Will. He drags me off of Fish.

I point at Fish, "You are weird."

Will looks crazy but Jack laughs bitterly, "Coming from her that is an insult."

I shake my head muttering, "I'm out of here. Friggin' insane bunch." I give Jack a look, "A couple guns and we're gone."

His eyes flicker to Fish, who is still in a daze of some sort. I almost feel sorry for him. He's lost his mind. I don't even know what's happening.

Fish waves a hand, "Give her guns and show her the way out." He turns and walks away. He's defeated, I think.

Jack looks confused or scared. He gives me a subtle headshake, "I told you to stay in the cabin."

I try really hard to give him a caring look, but I know how it looks on me. It always looks like I don't give a shit. I've mastered it. I turn and walk away. A man standing near the cabin gives me a wide birth as he walks past me. I almost feel like faking at him and watching him run away.

I see now that my way of reacting is never the same as other people's, except Will. Me and him react exactly the same, only he ends up calling me crazy and telling me how unstable I am. I snort and walk into the cabin where Star and Jake are talking quietly. I nod, "We're leaving now. Sleeping in the woods with nature would be better than trying to sleep here."

She looks exhausted but smiles, "Okay. We killing on the way out?"

I sigh, "I don't know. These guys are crazy."

Will comes in the cabin after me. He gives me a hard look. I sneer at him.

"They've been eating some of the people they kill."

I don't understand. I stand there confused and still for a minute. Jake and Star must be feeling the same way, because they don't say anything either. None of us move or speak for a minute.

Will nods, "I know."

I shake my head, "What? No. I must have misheard you."

His lip is tucked into a constant grimace, "No. They've eaten some humans. They got real hungry last winter. Jack had been doing the hunting but he wanted to find other folks to live with. He saw them all getting weird, like they had been alone too long. He knew they needed more diversity and he'd heard about the rebel camps having women and men. He figured these boys needed some women. When he left they caught a big bunch of men and a couple women. They had run out of meat..."

I put a hand up, "Stop."

He nods slowly, "We gotta go. Jack was gonna down a big deer or something to start a big barbecue up before we left. So that would be cooking as we left. Drinking and eating distracts them."

"That's why they're so strange?"

He gives me a look.

"They're eating people and Jack wants us to let some of them live? He thinks they'll be okay if Fish is dead?"

He nods once.

I storm past him, flinging the door open and scan the grounds.

I'm breathing like a crazed person. I see a crossbow like the one I had a few years back. I storm up to the guy next to it.

I point at it, "Can I have that?"

He gives me a look, "Get lost."

I punch hard, cracking his jaw and my hand. He's up and off his feet, but I have the crossbow in my hands. I point it at his chest, "I asked nicely."

He wipes the blood from his face, "You never said please. I see the blade in his hands come at me. I leap back, pulling the trigger. The arrow slices into his arm. He drops the blade as I kick his legs out from under him. Another guy gives me a look. I wing his right arm too. Grabbing the small stack of fresh arrows from the ground, I glance around at the fire pit. There is no one around.

The two guys I shot are calling me names but Will and Jake are with me. I hear scuffles and harsh words. I'm at my threshold for crazy.

I wish Leo were with me. Holding the crossbow up and taking small steps, I round the corner of the cabin where the guy was sitting. I fire three shots, hitting the three guys standing next to a smaller fire pit. The fire is being built by a forth guy. I miss him, reload and hit his right arm. Jack comes running when he hears the screaming. He points a gun at me, "Stop."

I shake my head, "Jack, me and you both know this is never going to stop."

I can feel Will's hulking body next to mine. I can hear the scuffles behind me. A gunshot makes me jump. I glance back at Star holding a handgun over a dead man. She has the dead look in her eyes. The man on the ground is the one who was mainly attacking her before.

I look at Jack, "You need to purge this place. It's only going to get worse."

His eyes shoot to his son. He's pleading with me, but I shake my head. He sighs, "Go, Emma."

I walk backwards, holding the crossbow on him, "How do we get out?"

He points, "Stay that way."

We start to the edge of the campground.

I hear a gunshot and turn to see another dead man on the ground. Star is walking away, turning her back on them. Jake and Will grab rifles and water bottles.

Jake reaches for some jerky on the picnic table but Will slaps it out of his hand, "Not from here."

We enter the woods and I hear the screams and gunfire continue. We break into a sprint, leaping logs and bushes. I know at least two are dead and five are hurt on their shooting arms. We run hard and fast.

Will is shouting at us to run harder. I look back for a second and see them running after us.

I leap for a large branched tree and scramble into it like a monkey. I sit fast and steady myself. The first guy goes down as he lifts his gun up. I take a deep breath and drop the second guy, just as he comes into view. He rolls on the ground, staring up at me with an arrow in his other eye. It's probably the best shot I have ever made, or luck. The third guy drops as I hear a gunshot. They start to fire on us, but we are better at this. We've had nothing but solid practice for months and haven't been drinking or eating people. Either way, we are a formidable team, minus Jake.

Jack and his son bring up the rear, shooting their own. I see Fish get a shot off. Jack drops into the woods. I leap from the branch and sprint into the group. Men are dropping all around me. I raise my crossbow and fire. Fish turns to me with a gun raised, just as the arrow hits his neck. He chokes but manages a shot. I don't feel the bullet. I'm certain it's missed me, but I hear a sound behind me. Someone making a noise like stumbling in the bush.

Jack's son is gone too. I get to Jack's body to see his son on his knees over his dying father. Jack smiles when he sees me, "Keep him safe for me."

I nod and grab his son by the arm. He is crying but lets me drag him away. I don't know how many are left. I don't know anything. I turn to drag the guy through the woods, but everything comes to a halt. A man holds a gun at me. I don't have time to react. The barrel is bigger than anything I've ever seen, like my eyes zoom in to see it. As it fires I'm shoved down into the bush. I hear a cry I recognize. I stop.

I'm frozen and I can't get air. Everything is gone in my world instantly. My plan, my hate, my revenge, my fears, and my loves, all fade away. If the sound of the person hurt is who I think it is. I look back over my shoulder to see Will leaning against a tree. The back of his tee shirt is red. I shake my head, "No." I run for him screaming, "NO!"

I can see that he isn't getting air. I don't know what to do. He drops to his knee, still hanging on the tree. I reach him, skidding on my knees and turning him to face me.

I grab his face, making him see me, "You need to make it to the vehicles. Okay?"

His breathing is fast and shallow. His eyes water and fill with panic, "Em, you okay?" His voice is gravelly, "You okay, baby?"

I cry and nod. He saved me. He is going to die for me. I'm not worthy of that. I run my hands down his cheeks, shaking my head.

I tear open the front of the shirt but there is nothing. I don't ever understand how he got shot in the back if he was shoving me to the ground. I spin him and see the jagged edge where the bullet went in. The wound is making a crackling sound with his shallow breaths. I look at my filthy hand and close my eyes. It's my best bet. I slap it against the bleeding wound and wrap my other arm around him. Jake grabs him from me.

"Oh shit. We need to run, let's go. We gotta get him to the city."

Jack's son gives me a look and nods, "Be right back."

He runs into the woods.

Jake looks at me for answers. I don't have any.

I grab Will and hug him, "It's okay." He can't sit still or talk. He's moving and trying so hard for air, I am dying inside. I want to breath for him.

Star is glossy-eyed and scared. She wraps her arms around him too. His face was red with the struggle to breathe but it's paler now, maybe from blood loss but not much is coming out. My heart is in my stomach, I'm sure. I stroke his head, "It's okay, we'll get you to the city."

Jack's son comes riding up on a horse, leading three others.

Jake points, "You get into the saddle and I'll pass him to you."

I ask, trying not to cry, "How far is the city?"

Jack's son shrugs, "A whole day's ride. But there is a town nearby. We can go there, they can help."

I shake my head, "No. The city is his best chance." I climb into the saddle. Jake lifts Will onto the saddle. I hold him tight. They mount. Jack's son starts fast. Star pulls her horse in next to mine, riding like she was born doing it. I would roll my eyes, if I wasn't so scared. She shouts, "I'm going for Bern. He'll get us to the city."

I swallow hard, thinking fast, "No. Don't go off alone." She waves, "Take care of him, Sis." She veers when we get to the road again and catches up to Jack's son. I can hear her shouting, but I can't pay attention to it. My butt is already killing me and my fingers are gripping to Will in the saddle in front of me. I don't recall exactly how to ride a horse. We're flopping in the saddle, and I feel like I'm going to lose him, but I hang on as hard as I can and ride.

Will is making terrible sounds but the wound isn't bleeding so badly. I don't know if that's a good thing.

We get to the bottom of the hill, and I watch as Star goes in a different direction than us. She gets smaller and smaller and I start to worry. Damn her for creeping into my 'us' but she's there.

We ride until every inch of me is aching but somehow numb. My body is killing me and my throat is burning. The horse seems like he's exhausted but he's working to keep up to the other two in the front.

I barely notice the scenery, or the fact the sun has gone down. I barely recall anything, but the sound of his breathing, and the way it's coming out the hole in his back.

Jack's son pulls back, "He okay?"

I shake my head, "I don't know." Will is bent over the front of the horse. I've pushed myself forward enough, that I'm holding him to the horse. My back is cramping, but I can't move or he'll fall off.

"The city is close."

I nod, "How long can the horse go for?"

"Not much longer."

I sigh and hold him to me, "Great. How long has it been since Star left?"

He shakes his head. I hold Will to me in desperation, as we make a dusty path behind us crossing the dry landscape. We don't see anyone, which is a bit odd.

"We must be close, no people. They always avoid the city."

I glance at Jake and nod. I wonder if my face has the same shell-shocked look as his, like there isn't any color left in us. His eyes are burning with anger and sorrow.

When I see the first building, I start to panic inside. Where is Star with Bern, and why aren't they with us yet? How will we get Will into the city?

I slide my pass out of my pants and glance at Jack's son, "Me and Will have a pass for the city. It's not real, but it worked last time. If I have to, I'll take him in alone."

Jake looks like he might argue but he knows it's Will's best chance. People in the borderlands don't have medicine to fix something like this.

We ride as hard as we can but our pace slows, as we get closer to the buildings. They loom over the tops of the trees ominously. I shudder when I think about the dead-eyed people, the breeder babies, and my father.

I get a flash of the gates through the trees as we get closer to the city. My heart is beating like I'm running through the woods; I feel sick but I keep the horse pointed in the right direction.

The heat of his body pressed against mine and the feel of his inconstant shuddering pushes me forward. I think he's near dead when I hear it. I turn to see a small truck rounding the corner. Sarah's little hand is waving from the window. We stop riding. I cling to Will as Bern stops the truck, skidding it along the broken pavement and dusty road. He, Star and Anna jump out, scared and running for me. I can't hear them. The blood is pounding in my ears now too. I know defeated tears are slipping down my cheeks, making their faces hazy. I don't know what to do, I want Bernie to solve this. Her hand grabs Will's leg with Jake and slides him from my arms. Cold shivers and screaming muscles take the place of the large man I've held to me for hours. I slip from the horse, collapsing on the ground. My whole body is exhausted beyond the point of being able to walk. Jake places Will in the back of the truck. Leo stands, still favoring his leg. He limps to me, nudging me to get up.

"Hey, boy." The thickness of his fur and the smell of him almost tempt me into a full-fledged crying fit. Instead, I let him help me up and walk me to the back of the truck. We limp together.

Sarah leaps at me after Will is situated. She cries silently; she's gotten so good at being quiet. I kiss the top of her head, "Hey, kid."

She sniffles, "Hi, Em."

Anna whispers, "What the hell?"

I shake my head, "I don't even have a way to explain." My eyes dart at Sarah. I can't explain anything in front of her. I can only hope Star filled them in. Star gives me a look. I nod at her, "Thanks."

She shakes her head, "You're part of my 'us' too, Em."

Anna wipes dust and dirt from her face; it's staining when it mixes with her tears. I drag myself into the back of the truck. Bernie is looking at the wound with a sour face, "Shit. How long has he been out?"

I nod, "A while."

He gives me a grim look, "We better get going then." He swallows hard, "Me, Anna, and Em are the only ones who can go. You all need to stay here. I'll come back for you. I have to get fuel in the city after I leave them there. I'll come back and bring you back to my place."

Jake crosses his arms, his eyes are red all around them, "No way. I'm coming too."

I shake my head, "We can't risk it. We need passes to get in."

He points at the wound, "We tell them we got ambushed and the bandits stole my ID."

I glance at Sarah and Star, lowering my voice, "I need you to stay with them."

He clenches his jaw. My eyes dart to Jack's son really quickly. He gets what I'm saying, thank God, and nods, "You hurry."

Leo jumps into the truck, but I shake my head, "You gotta stay with Sarah. She needs you."

His yellow eyes get confused and sad for a minute. I shake my head again, swallowing the lump in my throat; I hate that I keep leaving him. His lip twitches, flashing me a fang. I smile, "Don't even give me that face. You gotta stay with Sarah."

He looks at her as she wipes her face, and tries not to look at Will's still and bloody body. He makes his shitty wolf noise and gets out of the truck. His limp looks bad. I nod at Star, "Check that leg, k?"

She nods, "Be fast."

Bernie passes them weapons. It dawns on me that we are near the place where I killed the infected and Will was in the tree. I shudder and drag my exhausted body closer to his lifeless one. I lift his still face into my lap and press my back into the back of the cab. Bernie and Anna jump in the front seat. I rifle Will's pockets, finding the crinkled pass in his back pocket.

The truck pulls away from the other half of us still standing on the dusty road, looking lost.

Sarah drops to her knee, wrapping her arms around Leo's head.

I wish everything were different.

Chapter Five

The apartment isn't the same without Will there. I pace back and forth and wonder how Bernie lived in such a tight place before. The walls feel like they're closing in around me.

I hold myself and pace. Anna doesn't move. She stares out the window, like she doesn't know how to be in here either.

I walk to the kitchen, grabbing some sandwiches that Bernie brought us. He got the stuff from the stores supply place. I eat because I should. I know that if I'm going to be strong again, I need food. It's the same reason that I eat when I come upon berries, even if I'm not hungry, I know I need them.

Anna watches out the window and then turns to see me eating. She nods and holds a hand out. I bring her two. She stuffs one in her mouth, chewing the whole thing and swallowing like a snake.

I sigh, "You think it's close to being over?"

She shakes her head and gets up. She comes back with water for both of us.

The sun sets in front of the huge window in the living room. It makes the odd-looking city appeared to be on fire with the orange light.

My stomach is a ball of nerves, and I have the worst feeling I can imagine.

"It doesn't seem like the way it should have gone."

She nods slowly, not looking at me.

"It seems like we should have found the creepy baby killers and killed them for Meg, then killed my dad, and then went and started over. I don't even know how to make it right again. I don't care about the babies, and the people, and the suffering." My words are cold and they burn my tongue a little, but that can't make me care. I just don't.

I look at her, hating the dead stare on her face, like she knows he's dead and she's given up. I hate that I probably look like that too. I bite my lip and look out the window again, "When it's over, whether he makes it or not, we give up."

She looks at me hard, but I shake my head, "We give up, we walk away, and we say screw this. I don't wanna be some flashy crow, and I don't wanna have the responsibility of the whole of what's left on my shoulders."

She searches my face and nods, putting her pinky finger out like Meg always did. I wrap mine around it and shake them, "We go home and make a new life, and say forget the rest of them."

She doesn't whisper or try to say anything. She isn't a coward. She doesn't take that path ever; it will be her first time.

I nod, "I'm done losing people."

We sit on the odd couch that feels too stiff, like no one ever sat on it, and watch the sky get dark again, like it has for the three nights we've been here. All I can do is pray that Jake, Star, and Jack's son, who I still have not formally met, are taking care of Leo and Sarah. I need that to be the case. I feel spread so thin that there isn't room for me to worry about them too.

The door opens; it makes us both lift a revolver to the person walking in.

Bernie's eyes are red and tired. He nods, "He made it."

I sigh and hug Anna. My eyes are closed, forcing tears back into them. Anna sighs over and over into my hair.

I turn to face him, "What happened?" We hadn't seen Bernie since the first day we arrived. He brought us food and left again.

He grabs a sandwich and sits down on the other uncomfortable chair, "Infection of the lung, pneumonia, so they had to drain it. He's been pumped full of every kind of antibiotic and other stuff. They have amazing technologies here; it's the only thing that saved him." He sighs, "They have him in a drug-induced coma and on a respirator."

Anna frowns, "What does that mean?"

Bernie shakes his head, "He won't be leaving here for some time."

Something about his face, and the way he says it, makes me feel weird. I don't say anything, I wait for him to continue; I know he's going to.

He swallows his sandwich and leans over, taking Anna's water. He rubs his eyes, looking lost, "They know he's a rebel. The doctors from the breeder farm he was once in remembered him. They were there; they recognized him."

My throat feels swollen and dry.

He looks at me, "I told them I knew nothing of it and left him there in their custody."

I'm frozen but Anna jumps up, her whisper screams are savage. She sounds like the infected have surrounded us. Her raw, high-pitch wheeze looses the words and neither of us knows what she is saying.

She leaps at Bernie, slapping and wheezing. He wraps himself around her, cradling her. He whispers back, trying to soothe her. She has finally snapped.

I am still frozen, taking it all in, but there is a question I don't understand, "Why are they keeping him alive, if they know what he is?" It comes out as a whisper, hollow and detached.

Bernie's eyes lift from Anna. He licks his lips and closes his eyes, "They know who you are to him. Marshall made a deal to trade you and Will in for a pass to the city. He wanted in, not just because life was easier here, but also because he had plans to sabotage the breeder program from within. He knew the best way to kill the snake, was to cut the head off. Marshall made the deal for you and Will. He convinced them Will was the leader of the rebellion and the instigator of the attacks on the breeder farms. He told them he was Will's captive and the way Will originally escaped the breeder farm."

It just keeps getting worse.The pile is so big I don't have a solution for the things that are going wrong.

I get up and start pacing again.

"Do they know I'm here?"

He shakes his head, "They don’t know what you look like. They assume like your father, but you don’t, actually. You look like her."

My head snaps around, "You've seen her?"

He nods, "Yeah. Her picture is in the files—hers and Star's mom’s, and the other first ones."

I can't get my breath. It's getting caught in my throat.

Anna is running her hands over her face and shaking her head.

I put my hands up, "I need air, Bernie. I need air. I can't breathe in here. I need some air." I'm about to panic. I can feel it. It's like the dead bodies in the bags are lying on top of me again. I can't get past them.

Bernie takes my hand and Anna's in his and pulls us out the front door. He drags us to the door with the stairs on it and pulls us inside of it. We walk up the stairs until we reach a door at the top. He opens it and holds it open. Warm air rushes me as I step out onto the roof of the building. I walk to the edge and breathe, like it's the first time in years, or ever.

The wind feels like it's coming from every direction. I can't help but close eyes and put my hands out, and let it overwhelm me.

Plans and ideas are forming fast in my head, moving like a chain over a gear. I push them away; fight or flight isn’t going to save me this time. I need to be smarter than my father.

I glance at Bernie, "What was Marshall's plan and how do you know it?"

He gives me a confused look, "I was told Marshall's version he fed them, and I figured the rest out on my own. Marshall and Will escaped the breeder farm with a doctor named Herbert Langdon. Langdon died in the escape, but told Marshall that his brother

Clyde worked in the city, for the planners. Will told me this years ago. We never thought much about it, not thinking we were going to destroy the city, or maybe just kill your dad. Long and short of it, I went to see Clyde. Marshall had him give him plans and weak points and a few other things. He said Marshall had a place in the city. Between Clyde and the doctor's stories, I have pieced it together."

I process it and look out at the night settling in over the city, "Did you tell Clyde, Marshall was dead?"

He scoffs, "No. That would be dumb. I told him we were here to put Marshall's plan into action. He told me to wait two days; that's what he needed to evacuate the people on our side from the city."

I glance at him, "He plans on destroying the city?"

He nods.

Anna whispers, "Then the bombs must be here already."

Bernie nods again, "Yup. He must have everything here and be ready to roll. I assume it's all in his place. We just need to find where he lived."

I shake my head, "Impossible. This place is massive."

"I know, but I have an in; I wrote the program to keep track of residents. It keeps track of health checkups and incidents. Everyone has a residence listed."

It almost feels hopeful, but then I remember Will, "How do we get Will out of here?"

He sighs, "That's the hitch. They expect you to come for him. They expect you to break into the city. They said the guards have been upped on the gates and the perimeters, and people in the streets are being checked."

Anna gives me a look, "Do they think we are with Will, since we came in with him?"

He shakes his head, "Our only saving grace is that I came in twice, for whatever reason, only my second entrance was recorded. The guard who let the four of us in, didn't record us. He only recorded when I came in alone two days ago, after I went and took Star and everyone home."

It seems too perfect. It feels like it breaks one of my rules. I shake my head, "We need to get out of here. It's too convenient. We need to go. Me and Anna will stay up here. You go find the address for Marshall's and then we all leave."

He shakes his head, "I can get it in the apartment. I have a computer that is linked, I work from home a lot."

He walks to the door, but I have the feeling in my guts that I have learned to trust, "Wait."

He looks back, "What?" He's getting annoyed.

I point, not really at him, but not away from him either, "If you brought Will in twice now, saved Anna once, and brought me in a few times, then you're linked to us. I bet you are being watched. Why would they trust you?"

His eyes look scary for the first time ever. He bites his lip, "Trust me, they just do."

I shake my head, "I want answers. This is too easy."

Anna looks confused.

He looks at her and then down, "This place wouldn't be possible without me. I knew exactly what they had planned from the start. I was young and stupid, and the idea made sense. I helped them make this place. The scientific proof was there. The UN was right, we were making the world sick. We were the problem. I was nineteen and it all made sense. The first paper I ever wrote in university was based on the UN's belief that the five-percent plan was the only way to save the world. Only I didn't stop there, I went on to help plan exactly how it would be implemented, ensuring only the best of the best survived to help weed out the imperfections. I was fourteen at the time. I went to university early."

I take a step back from him, "Bernie." Anna looks like she might get sick.

He nods, "I'm not proud. They recruited me when I was turning nineteen. I had a double doctorate. I didn't know that some of my teachers were members of the special committee formed by the UN to plan this out." He sighs, "I saw the Georgia Guidestones as a kid. I saw them and I believed that they were correct. The science was there. So when they explained what was about to happen, I believed."

I give Anna a look and then him, "What's a guidestone?"

She shakes her head, but he gets a gleam in his eye.

"In the seventies, a man using an alias commissioned a monument in Elbert County, Georgia. The monument was made of granite and stood almost twenty feet high. It's got an inscription on it that's translated into eight modern languages and four ancient ones. The inscription is ten principles or guides to a successful future."

I sit down on the ledge of the roof, "This is about to get creepy, isn't it?"

He nods, "It is. Rule one, maintain humanity under 500,000,000 in perpetual balance with nature. Rule two, guide reproduction wisely—improving fitness and diversity. Rule three, unite humanity with a living new language. Rule four, rule passion—faith—tradition—and all things with tempered reason. Rule five, protect people and nations with fair laws and just courts. Rule six, let all nations rule internally resolving external disputes in a world court. Rule seven, avoid petty laws and useless officials. Rule eight, balance personal rights with social duties. Rule nine, prize truth—beauty—love—seeking harmony with the infinite. Rule ten, be not a cancer on the earth—leave room for nature—leave room for nature."

Anna whispers, "You repeated the last part."

He nods, "Yup. That's exactly as it's stated on the guidestones. So the plan was implemented, all nations would adhere to this but keep their countries pure to whatever they were initially. Blacks were sent to Africa, South Americans to South America, Chinese to China, and so forth."

I point at his face, "There were Americans and Canadians who were born here and white people who were born in Europe, how did you sort that out?"

He shakes his head, "We didn't—are you kidding? We lost total control. The infection was based on something that could be cured and prevented in the right people, genetically-superior people. It didn't work. It mutated. We had to build the city, try to keep the people we were breeding alive, and Michael was slowly getting crazier and crazier."

I wave my hand, "I don't want to know. I change my mind; I don't want to know."

He sighs and gives Anna a defeated look, "I'm sorry. You now that's not how I think now, right?"

She shrugs and looks down. I can see the fury on her and she's unstable enough to act out on it. I point to the door, "Let's go find Marshall's plan and end this shit."

He looks sickened, but not nearly as much as we are. I knew how it worked, essentially, but not to this degree. One language and prizing beauty with truth and love, that's crazy. Beauty is nothing, compared to truth and love.

I walk down the stairs, unsure of Bernie's true feelings. I know Anna feels the same way I do. I can tell by the way she's walking close to me and glancing back. He leads us to the door to his place.

"Just give me a second." He goes in first, alone, and comes back minutes later, "I know where Marshall's is."

We leave the apartment doorway, and walk to the door to the garage. I hate the garage; it's still as dark as night in there. I can't see a thing. Anna stays close to me, "This place is creepy," she whispers.

I nod, not that she can see it, "Yup."

Bernie's hand reaches for mine, as we get further into the darkness, "It's this way," he whispers.

I don’t know how he can tell, it's so black everywhere. Suddenly, light floods the area as he opens a door. It's a stairwell. He steps in and the lights shift. It's those annoying lights that only turn on when you walk under them. I point upward as they shift with our steps, "These were a stupid idea."

He snorts but continues down the flights of stairs. When we reach the bottom, he grabs Anna and does the first bold thing I have ever seen. He plants his lips on hers, muttering into the kiss, "I don’t care about any of this. I love you, and if you can't love me anymore, just kill me."

In the flickering light, I see they are the same. They don’t take the coward’s path, like I do. She shakes her head, whispering into him. His lips turn up and I can't stop staring at them both. My heart is so broken, I know I'll never live through this. My stomach hurts all the time but this makes it worse.

I know in the flickering light that I would pick him, every time it would be him. Even if he dies, it will still be him. I open the door and walk past them.

I need the fur in my fingertips, and the mean stares from the man I love, to make all of this go away. Hell, even that little, saucy blonde is part of the things I need.

What I have though, is a mute psycho and a slightly-crazy genius and no plan whatsoever.

Bernie mutters to me as he walks past me, "Follow me."

Anna catches up to me, looking slightly more blushed and peaceful. She glances at me sideways but doesn't say anything. I don’t care. I trust Bernie; even if I don’t want to, I do. We walk in peace until I notice she's glancing around. I whisper, "You have to keep your eyes up and look straight ahead—they don’t look around or talk to each other."

She shakes her head, "I don't like it here."

"Me either."

Bernie stops after a while in front of the only building I think doesn't look like the others. The doorway is old and arched. It looks like it has character and has been weathered in a different way or time than the rest of the other buildings.

Bernie swipes the door, opening it for us.

"Is this older than the rest of the city?"

He nods as he closes the door, "This is the only thing left of Newport, Washington. Safest place in the USA. Close to fresh water, four seasons, no threat of flood or drought, low population, so we could get them out and take over the town with very little concern to the rest of the world, and natural barriers. The coastal mountains held off a lot of the tidal waves and the Rockies prevent anything from coming from the other side. Not too south so as to be too hot, and not too north, to be too cold. The watershed is replaced every year by the snowfall, and yet, it's dry and warm in the summer for farming. Perfection."

I look around the old foyer of the building, "What's this?"

He grins, "The old court house. We set up here in the beginning while we were taking over the town."

I shake my head, "If only you had put that much effort into saving the world."

He scoffs, "We did try, don't ever let anyone tell you we didn't try." I think I've annoyed him. He climbs the stairs to the second floor. We walk down the dark hall in silence. He stops in front of a door but drops to his knees. He gets close to the handle and I hear metal lightly tapping against itself. He opens the door a second later. A smell creeps out into the hallway as the door opens fully. I step back, pulling my gun from the back of my pants. I step softly into the room, smelling and listening but there is nothing. It's silent as whatever is dead in there.

My animal eyes switch on, the room is still. I open the fridge and close it quickly, "It's the old food. He hasn't been here in a while."

Bernie closes the door, switching on a small light in the living room. We search the cupboards. I want to take the food but I know that's not why I'm here. I close the cupboard, leaving behind weeks' worth of perfectly-good food. That bothers me. We search every room methodically. I find a book called The Da Vinci Code and stuff it into my pocket. Anna grins when she sees it. We meet back in the living room and sit on the couches. I glance at Bernie, "You find anything at all?"

He shakes his head, "No. Marshall was too smart for that, I guess."

That doesn't make me feel better. We are running low on time. When Will is well enough to wake, he's going to be tortured to find me. That is something I will not allow to happen.

I tap my fingers against the couch and stare out the dirty window, "It really doesn't look like he was ever here."

"I know."

Anna nods and pulls the book out of my pocket. She flips to the first page, making me smile. I have created a monster. My foot starts tapping, joining in with my fingers. The floor echoes my tapping, making Bernie sit up. He flops off the couch to his knees and crawls to the spot I'm tapping. He knocks on the floor in a big circle. One spot sounds hollow, compared to the others. He gets up and rushes to the kitchen. He comes back with a knife and skids along the floor to the spot again. He stabs the knife into the floor, picking at the wood. A chunk of wood shoots off, leaving a small opening. He picks at the floor and sticks his hand in the hole. He sighs and pulls out a piece of paper and looks at it quizzically.

"What does it say?"

"Black lab stop HEMP stop Kansas stop."

I furrow my brow, "Is that English?"

He laughs, "It's sent like it's a telegram."

I shake my head, "A what?"

He laughs harder. Anna is biting her nails and reading, ignoring us completely.

He bites his lip and looks at the words like they're magically going to make sense and then sighs, "Shit."

"What's a telegram?"

He sighs, "It was a way of sending and receiving messages, back in the day, before phones and internet and everything."

"What's it trying to stop?"

He looks confused, " What?"

I point at the paper, "The stops—what's it stopping? How do you stop Kansas?"

"No, it's where you stop talking. End of the sentence. So this says, Black Lab, HEMP, Kansas."

I stand up and pace again. I feel like that's all I do indoors. "Where is the black lab?"

He shakes his head, "Not a clue, but I know what a HEMP is and where Kansas is." He stands and paces too, "EMP stands for electromagnetic pulse and the H is for high altitude. It's a way to shut down all electricity and power. The layman's way of describing it is it's a nuclear-powered missile, essentially with capability to destroy everything electric and battery powered. Nothing would work. It was a way of shutting everything down in a country you wanted to destroy. The civilization we lived in was completely dependent upon electricity and technology. This was a warfare that didn't kill people, it killed the machines we needed."

I sit again, "Wait, so Marshall thought there was one of these in Kansas?"

He nods, "I would have to assume he felt that way and wrote this down for someone to find or to remind himself that's where it was, or someone else put it here for him to find."

I point at him, "That's got to be it. He never had time to come here."

He nods, "Well then, I would have to say, he was going to Kansas to detonate this missile in something called the black lab, and he was going to ruin the breeder farms with it."

I frown, "How far is Kansas?"

He sighs, "Far, very far."

"That doesn't make sense. All the way to Kansas to destroy this city? That must be a code. I had heard about codes before."

Bernie stands and looks out the window, "Only one person will know that."

I nod, "The minute we ask, he's going to know we aren't who you said we were."

He turns for the door, "I'll be back."

He closes the door and I stare out the window, chanting HEMP, Black Lab, and Kansas until the words don't even sound like words anymore.

Chapter Six

The door flies open. Bernie looks a little crazed with blood smears on his lips and a swollen eye, but the guy lying on the ground looks much worse.

He leans in the frame, grinning at us, "Clyde, this is Emma and Anna."

I smirk, "I didn't see that coming."

Anna frowns from halfway through her book and stands up. Bernie looks beat in every way. He points, "Can you get the answers from him? I'm more of a tech guy."

I nod and crouch down to the older man who's giving me a hesitant look.

"What is the black lab?"

He spits at me. I can take a lot of things, but I do not like to be spit at. I smack his face into the wooden floor and then haul him up, bloody nose and all. I slam him into a cupboard, "What is the black lab?"

He starts to laugh, "You can't stop us. We're everywhere. God made sure of that."

I roll my eyes and look at Bernie, "You didn't tell him that we want to make it end? That we're on the same team?"

Bernie shook his head, "He wouldn't let me talk."

I give Clyde a smile, "We want the same thing as you."

He growls, "I know what you are—you're sin and temptation from the devil himself."

I'm not sure I have a response for that, so I punch him in the throat hard. It seems like the right thing to do. He gags and heaves, struggling for air. I drag him over to the curtains, tear them down, and kick him onto the couch. I push his arms behind his back and wrap him in the curtain, so his fingers stick out the bottom of the wrap. I pull my knife from my boot and stab it into the base of his finger, "Where is the black lab?"

He screams, but I press his face into the couch. I can hear gasps from Anna and Bernie, mostly Bernie, but I press the knife in deeper. He cries out, as the first finger is gone. It's only his pinky; he doesn't need it, not really.

"Where is the black lab?"

"I'll t-t-t-tell y-y-y-you, j-j-j-just stop."

I cut into the meat of the second finger. He screams, "U-u-under th-th-the main lab. Under Michael's l-l-lab."

I frown, "What's Kansas?" I ask and cut at the same time, shoving his face into the pillows.

"Stop, Emma. Let him talk."

I ignore Bernie. Anna can deal with him.

I cut into the knuckle a bit more.

"It's the detonation location! It'll level all of the USA! The missile has to detonate there!" He screams but the pillow muffles it. I drop him to the ground, "If you hurry to the hospital, they can sew that one back on. I heard that anyway."

He cries, "Screw you, crazy bitch." Spit and blood pours out of his face as he cries. I grimace and look at Bernie, "How self-explanatory is a nuclear bomb?"

He can't tear his eyes from Clyde, but he answers, "Not at all. I have to come with you."

I glance at Anna, "You keeping him company?" I nod at Clyde. She nods and shrugs, "I can finish my book." Her look darkens, "You gonna get Will first?"

I try to smile, but I know what's going to happen. Her face

hardens, "Can you try?"

I want to cry but I don't. I nod, "I will do everything I can to save him."

She looks down so I barely hear the whisper, "I know you will."

Bernie looks grey, "You didn't have to go so hard."

I ignore him and let my cold hate and fear make me what I used to be, what my father intended me to be all along. We get back onto the street where I stick my bloody knife back in my boot and wipe my hands on my pants.

Bernie grimaces, "You are disturbing."

I give him a sideways glare, "I'd hate for you and my dad not to get your money's worth."

He sighs, "It wasn't supposed to be like that." He turns and walks, taking me with him.

"It's quiet tonight."

He nods, "They expect you to attack the gates any second, I think."

"You all are too confident. That's your problem. You think you can fix what God made, but you think you're smarter than him, so you can take the easy route. He put some serious effort into this place."

He looks back at me, almost mocking me, "God? Really?"

I narrow my gaze, "Yeah, God. I believe. If Meg is dead, then there is a God and she is up there arguing with him right now. He is getting a 'my momma' talk as we speak."

He chuckles, "Touché."

I don't know what that means, but I'm too tired and scared to care. My body is so tightly wound, that I don't know what to do with myself. I know how it's going to end;, Will is going to die, and I'm not sure I can live with that.

"This is the building."

We stop in front of the building we went to last time. He scans us in and walks inside. A guard walks up right away, "Hey Bernie!"

Bernie smiles and points at me, "Good evening. This is my colleague from one of the farms. She's here to see about some drugs we've been working on."

The guard gives me an uncertain look. I walk towards him with my hand out, like a civilized person. Of course he sees the old bloodstain and frowns. I kick his legs out, duck from the blow he's about to deliver, and punch his stomach. He buckles so I can wrap my arm around his throat. I drop back, breaking his neck. Bernie gags slightly, looking disturbed, "What the hell?"

I drag the guard behind the front counter and take his gun, listening for everything else that could attack.

We sneak through the building, with the lights overhead flashing and announcing us. I give Bernie a look. He puts his hands up, "I know, I know. These were stupid."

I mutter and climb the stairs.

He glances at me, "You ever feel bad, Em… for killing them?"

I shake my head, still listening to the stairwell as we walk along.

He looks confused, "Why not?"

I want to say wolves raised me and laugh, but I don't. My heart is in my throat and everything is burning. I don't know what to expect or find, but I know I need to see him once before we end everything in the whole world for good. I give Bernie a shrug, "I don't think of them as people; they're obstacles." I take another step, "It's us or them, and I choose us every time."

He nods and turns back around, "Glad I'm in the 'us'."

I don't say anything else, hoping he shuts up. He stops outside of a doorway and nods, "Same as last time. You ready?"

I shake my head. It's true, I'm not. I'm scared of losing the thing I can't live without.

He points, "I'll go first, stay close and the lights will come on for me, not you. Okay?"

He swipes and enters the large lab. The lights flick on, but we don't get two steps before a man comes up to Bernie, "What are you doing here?" He's older with a gray beard. He's not my father, I can tell.

Bernie nods back at me, "You all are acting crazy tonight. This chick told me I wasn't allowed to come in the building unaccompanied. I told her I don't need a guard, but she won't listen."

The man glances at my gun and nods, "She's right. We are on lock down. The prisoner we have back there is Michael's."

Bernie sighs, pinching the bridge of his nose, "I guess I have to tell you too. Michael wants him injected with a 3507. He wants to be able to track him. He asked me to come do it."

The man looks confused, "A tracker? Why? The man's in a coma. He ain't going anywhere."

Bernie tilts his head, "That group of rebels may come and take him; Michael is sure they'll try the city gates tonight."

The man steps aside, "Just be fast. I don't want anyone up here tonight." He gives me a look, "You stay with him."

I nod, confused at his gullibility. These people have lived safely in these walls too long. Morons.

Bernie walks us both to the back of the room. He scans the lab door, opening it for me. My gut kicks in when I see Will lying on the table. He's relaxed and clean again, naked from the waist up, with a large, white bandage on his chest.

When the door closes, I take a step towards Will but Bernie makes a noise, "No miss, you stand over to the side, please. I don't want you interfering with my work."

I can tell by his tone, we are being watched. I step to the side, pressing my back against the wall and waiting as he grabs a huge needle from the case. He leans over the computer next to the case and starts typing. The seconds feel like hours. The ten feet between me and Will feel like miles. His breath is funny and forced. The machine next to him makes his chest lift and fall. It makes him live.

Bernie stands, grabbing the huge needle and glances at me, "Come hold his arm down, just in case."

I know it's the moment he's giving me to say goodbye.

I lay my gun against the wall and take the couple steps I need to, to be next to his bed. Hesitantly and slightly shaky, I lift my fingers to his forearm, holding his warm skin in my hands for what might be the last time. His stern smile flashes in my eyes, but I push it away.

Bernie leans across him with the needle, "He may jump, hold him down."

I nod, gripping tighter.

Will makes a funny noise, tossing his head a little. His eyes flutter for a second and hope fills me, but then he settles back in. Bernie injects the huge needle into his arm. Will tenses. I hold him still, fighting my tears.

I feel like a thousand whispers pass between my fingers and his arm. A thousand things I needed to say, or just one maybe. One thing to make sure he knows. I nearly lower my face onto his chest and close my eyes; he's become my human Leo. I can sob into his chest just like Leo's and feel the same safety and comfort. His arms wrap around me the same way. He makes the world be quiet for a minute.

I squeeze once more and a subtle smile creeps across his lips.

Bernie pulls the needle out. I don’t move though. I hold his arm, like it's the only thing stopping me from going nuts.

Deep down, I know nothing is going to stop me when he's gone. I'll kill everyone. I know that.

Bernie smiles like he's about to sell me something, "Okay, let's go."

He walks to the door. I let go of Will, turning my back slowly, and try not to feel every step.

Bernie closes the door, leaving nonchalantly.

The lights flick on, leaving it dark behind us where the door was.

The man with the gray beard walks towards us, constantly in the light as they switch on for him too.

"All done?"

Bernie nods, "Yup. Have a good night, Frank."

"Night, Bernie."

We get into the stairwell and Bernie slumps against the wall. He takes a huge breath, "Okay. We gotta find that HEMP."

I frown, "What did you inject him with?"

He grins, "A 3507. Now if they try taking him anywhere, we can find him."

"Is that going to hurt him?"

He shakes his head, "No."

We walk down the stairs, "Where is this black lab?"

He looks back, "I think it's across the street. Michael's got a secret lab he thinks none of us know about. I didn't know it was called the black lab. The HEMP is under the lab, I guess." He jogs down the stairs, shouting back at me, "I assumed it was where he was making his monsters. I sort of lost interest in that, after I started seeing the mess we were making."

I grip the gun tighter and follow him to the bottom of the stairs. He stops and smirks, "I wonder…" He walks to a door, swiping his pass at the scanner. It doesn't open. He gets a grin on his face, and drops to his knees, and pulls something from his pocket. He works on the scanner for a minute and then scans his pass again.

The door opens. He gives me a look, "Kill anyone we see in here, that's our only option."

I nod and walk in after him. He says it all grim and frightened, but I planned on that anyway. I don't tell him that. He already looks at me like I'm scary; we don't need to make it worse. I pass him my gun, "Don't shoot unless I say shoot."

He swallows and nods. I pull my bloodstained knife out of my boot and creep ahead in the long corridor. It's narrow and lit with sporadic, round wall lights. They are dim and orange, and remind me of the light in Brian's bunker. I grip the knife, creeping along the wall, listening to everything and nothing, all at once. I don't like narrow hallways, I decide this now. I like the openness of the forest. This feels like I might never escape or the walls are going to close in on me. Bernie's careless footsteps are the thing I hear until a cough fills the silence. I put a hand up, halting Bernie.

I glance around the corner ahead of me, seeing a man with a gun and his hand against his lips. He coughs again and leans into the wall. I tuck the blade behind my back and walk toward him slowly, not making any sounds. He yawns and closes his eyes for a second. I almost stop and wait for him to open his eyes, but the coward in me pushes on. I pull the blade softly, not making a sound, and swing it wide as I reach him. His eyes fly open, but it's too late. His jugular is hit. He drops his gun, but I catch it as he slumps along the wall, bleeding out. I sling the rifle over my shoulder and tiptoe further down the hall. I reach a door and look back at Bernie. He pulls out the screwdriver he had before and drops to his knees, fiddling with it like the other one. He scans and the door unlocks. I push it open, peeking around the corners for movement. The area is completely dark. I step in and the light flicks on above me.

"I hate this city."

Bernie closes the door, standing under the light with me. The hallway only goes one way, so I walk ahead with the lights announcing me to anyone who is ahead. I can't see into the black oblivion of the rest of the hallway.

My breath speeds up with my heartbeat. I don't know that we're in the right place, or that we'll see anything that helps. I don't know if that was the last time I'll ever see Will alive. I don't know anything, but that my feet don't want to take any more steps, and my heart is aching like there is no tomorrow. Granny used to say that, 'like there is no tomorrow.'

I stop when the lights show a door. Bernie opens it and closes it, "No."

We move ahead, keeping a close eye on the darkness, and the fact it isn't moving or making noises.

My body hair is standing on end. I have a disturbing feeling that the infected are going to pop out any second. They always manage to when it's dark and creepy and you're lost. They may be brain dead, but they have an uncanny ability to time their arrivals.

My hands start shaking as I round another corner. Bernie is opening every door he sees, but is still moving along behind me. I reach the end of the hallway and glance back at him. In the white light of the spotlight, I see the frustration on his face. I feel it too.

We're wasting time. Will could be dying upstairs, Anna could be getting discovered, or Jake and Sarah could be fighting for their lives at the house. He sighs and messes with the scanner on the door and opens it. There is a flight of stairs before us. The lights are the dim, orange, round ones—thank God.

Bernie smiles, "About time." He walks ahead into the dim light and looks down over the edge of the metal staircase. It looks flimsy, and when we step on it, our steps echo.

I shake my head, "I don't like this."

He shakes his head, "Me either." He starts down the stairs, but I grab his arm, "Let me go first."

I slip past him, wiping sweat from my brow. My footsteps are slightly quieter than his on the metal stairs. I walk toe first, looking down over the edge the entire time.

A red light starts to flash above our heads when we're halfway down. I look back at Bernie, "We've been discovered."

He frowns, "How do you know?"

I point at the flashing light, "Same alarm as the breeder farms."

He shrugs, "That goes off all the time. Random things make it go off."

I shake my head, "Not when I'm around; it's always me." I start to run down the stairs, wishing Leo was with me. His senses don't get messed up by the buildings, he's a wolf through and through. I'm only a wolf in the woods. My eyes and senses are distracted by the building closing me in.

When I get to the bottom of the stairs, I see a panel and steam just like the boiler room at the farms. My belly starts to ache. I lift the rifle, looking around the room. Pipes and bits of machinery make up the room. The walls are dank with sweat from whatever these things are and the heat they're making.

Bernie walks to the panel, lifting a screen and turning something on. The light from it makes a new brightness in the orange glow and the flashing red lights. I think I might go crazy waiting for the dart gun or the real gun to hit me. I know it's an ambush; it feels like the one set for me with Marshall.

Bernie starts typing fast.

"Jesus. This thing is legit. It's old as hell, but it's legit."

I glance back at him, "How long?"

He shakes his head, "I just need to break the codes and launch it."

I sigh, "How long, Bern?"

"Ten minutes, maybe."

I sigh, "Shit." Ten minutes will feel like forever.

His fingers fly across the clunky keyboard. He wipes away sweat, almost in sync with me. The room feels like a steam bath like the one I went to with Granny. We were staying in a hotel in Vegas once. Granny wanted to go there so bad and Lenny said no, so she waited until he was gone on one of his trips and took me then. Just like she let me use her ereader, got me an Xbox, and let me play on her laptop, she let me be a normal kid when Lenny wasn't there. Looking at the clunky, old laptop I barely recall how to use it.

Bernie shakes his head, "I can't believe they put this here. I can't believe I never knew."

"Why did they?"

He shrugs, "Not a clue. Must be the fail safe, in case the wrong people get control again, or if another country comes to invade, I guess. We did this to every other country, so the threat of them coming for us was never a real one."

I scowl, "You did what?"

He gives me a blank stare, "We launched HEMP's over everyone. We killed the power grids in every country but ours."

I shake my head, "What about the cities? Will said that the other cities were like this one. Every continent had cities, there were ten or something."

He shakes his head too, "No. We wanted to end world wars and pollution, and we did. We were scared they would launch these over us, so we removed all threats."

I feel weird about the fact he knew they did this to other places, "Is this something you had planned to maybe do to the United States?"

He shakes his head, "No. I didn't even know there was a contingency plan in place here. It makes me uncomfortable to know they had one for the breeder farms. It means they have fully lost control of the virus, with no possibility of getting it back."

The talk of the infected, combined with the flashing red lights, makes me considerably more uncomfortable. "Do you think the newer breeder babies are really immune?"

He shakes his head, "I don't know what to think. I'm not a

virologist. I'm a tech nerd..."

A noise cuts him off. We both freeze, except for his fingers. They continue to type. I scan the top of the stairs as I hear another noise.

"Bernard? Really?"

I know the voice instantly, as the face I barely recall hovers over the railing. "And you must be Emma. You look so much like her, it's frightening."

My stomach drops.

Bernie's fingers don't stop but he speaks softly, "Michael, meet your daughter."

He laughs and shakes his head. He looks nearly identical to my father, but older and more tired. His eyes gleam, "You've been causing me some serious issues."

He starts down the next flight of stairs. I walk up them, glancing back at Bernie, "Don't stop."

He nods, wiping more sweat from his brow.

I take the stairs two at a time. Michael stops walking, pausing and listening, "Bernard, stop that. You'll never break the code on that one."

I round the corner to the next flight but stop; he's there in all his glory. I've made him into a huge monster, but I see he's no larger than any other man I've killed with my bare hands.

He smirks at me, "You must have so many questions."

I watch his eyes, making certain I can see the plotting behind them. He takes a step towards me. I don't move but his steps are timid. He's scared of me. He knows what I'm capable of.

"Emma, you were one of the first. We had twenty women come in, six of the babies died. The mothers of the ones who lived got very sick. The babies are too strong of a parasite and the immune systems we gave them were unstoppable. You could inject HIV into a Gen child and they will kill the disease. Your bodies actually destroy cancer cells when they try to form inside of you. I can inject your blood into people and it will fight disease and infection."

I hardly listen to him. I listen for the fingers typing and watch for the movement in his eyes.

"You are magnificent. God himself would bow before what I have created."

He puts a hand out for me to take, "I can show you the others like you. You can teach them how to control what they are and how to manage their moods and tempers. I know you can do it. The ones from the beginning are the special ones. We made the rest from you, from your DNA." He starts to laugh maniacally, like a cartoon character. I hear a gunshot and look over the edge at Bernie slumping over the keyboard. A man behind him with a gun pointed at his back looks up at me.

His eyes are so busy searching mine for the despair I know is there, that he misses the fingers reaching for the keyboard. He misses the determination in Bernie and assumes he's dead. But I know Bernie. I know his goal in life is to stop this. I only let my peripheral gaze see the hand press the last buttons, almost silently. I deadlock his gaze to mine as Bernie's fingers flutter over the keyboard. He presses the last buttons and the red flashes become sounds. The man's gun goes off again, but it doesn't matter. Whatever Bernie did, it's done. I look up at Michael's face. His cocky smile fades. He rushes past me to the basement floor shouting, "STOP IT!"

The man dives for the keyboard but the beeping alarm and the flashing lights don't end.

Tears threaten my vision. I see a countdown on the screen. The numbers look like it might be a minute. I break into a run, a sprint. My lungs are screaming for air in the dank room as they mix with a panic attack, and the possibility that I won't make it. I have a new plan, but I don't know if it's enough. I run through the door to the hallway and sprint harder. The door to the far hallway is ajar with a boot. In the dim, orange light, I can see it's from the dead man on the floor. I snatch his pass and run for the far side of the dank corridor.

I don't hear anything but my heartbeat.

She can't lose Bernie and Will. I can't do that to her. I run harder, getting back into the other building. The stairs and the passes can't go fast enough. My legs burn as I reach the lab where I know Will is.

I fling open the door and run across the floor. The lights can barely keep up with me but as I near the door to his room, I see the man with the gray beard. He points a gun at me, "Where is Bernie?"

I shake my head, sniffling almost and heaving for air, "He's dead. Michael killed him." I'm hoping he's on our side.

He nods, keeping the gun on me, "Good news."

I see his finger tense to pull the trigger, but there is a sparking noise and the lights cut out. We stand in the darkness for a second before I see the spark of light from the gun. I've moved but he doesn't know that. He doesn't know I can move silently. He doesn't know I can see in the dark better than he can. When my hand grabs his forehead and my knife slices across his throat, he doesn't know his death is seconds away.

I hold him tight, waiting for him to move his hands and fire the gun, but he drops to the floor. I feel around in the dark for his gun and take it from his still-warm, gripping hand. For whatever reason, that bothers me. I turn and run for the door. I have to feel in the dark for the handle. The scanner doesn't work and the door won't open.

Frustrated, defeat starts to build but I refuse. The tears have started, but through them I feel for the place where the door clicks shut. I place the barrel of the gun on that spot and angle my body away from it. I fire but the door still won't open. I kick at it but it won't open. I drop to my knees, screaming and pounding on it. He's in there dying alone; the life support has cut off. I cut the power with Bernie and he's in there without me. He's dying without me. Bernie is face down in the basement with my screaming father, and I'm stuck in the lab with a dead man and my heart breaking.

I wipe my face and stand, turning the handle and kicking again. I hear the door make a noise and do it again. It makes another noise. My leg feels like it might break, but I kick once more, snapping something inside of the door. It flies open. I rush in, hands out.

I can't feel anything and I'm scared they took him away. The tracer won't work to find him. They've moved him and I've lost him.

"Will, baby you here? Will?"

I trip and fly across the room. My hands land on the edge of the bed as I fall. I grip it, scrambling to my feet and slapping down on him the entire way. His body is there. I think it's him. I run my hands up his bare chest to the bandage; it's him. I drag my hands along his face to where the tube is in his nose and the mask is on his face.

He's warm but the machines aren't moving. I pull the mask off slowly, trying not to shake when I move my fingertips. I flip the nose thing out of his nostrils. His face is slack. I kiss his cheek, whispering, "Baby, don't leave me. Please, Will. Don't leave me."

I don't know, nor care, where Michael is. I don't know if I will make it out of the city, or if anything is ever going to be okay in this world with nothing. All I need to know is how to save him. I kiss his face again and part his lips. I breathe into his mouth. I remember first air. Mouth to mouth was not as important as chest compressions. I remember that. I feel for his heart and push down but the bed is too soft, it doesn't compress.

I cry louder, "Will, goddammed don't leave me." I breathe into his lips again but nothing happens. I feel his arms for the plastic lines of the I.V. I saw before.

I need light. I feel around for the counters I saw. When I open a drawer I can't tell what anything is. I drop to my knees again, pulling more drawers open, but I still don't recognize anything. Everything I touch is a foreign object.

My hands shake, blood makes them sticky, but I still search each drawer, not knowing what I'm looking for.

I pass over things, as if any of it is going to help. There is a driving need to touch every drawer and every item, as if one might tell me it's the thing I need.

I reach the bottom drawer and still no answers. The plan I had, depended on light still being in the room or Bernie being with me… or both. I close my eyes, not that it makes a difference, and take a breath. I am defeated.

I crawl along the floor to his bedside. I drag my hands up the frame of the bed, clutching to the bedding and then to him. I lean my head against the cold railing and sob. I don't have anything else. I have no Leo, Anna, Meg, Star, Bernie, or anyone to make a difference. Don't even have Jake to just be there. It's just like before. I'm ten years old and totally alone in the dark.

I grip to his arm, holding tight. If I let go, he's gone forever. I press my lips against his hand and let the tears wash over me.

Chapter Seven

My footsteps are clumsy on the stairs. My hand squeals along the metal railing as I slip a little. I'm out of bullets and I don't know if the door at the bottom is open or not. I just walk down the stairs. Something gleams off of the railing when I round a corner. There is light at the bottom of the stairs somewhere.

"Hello?" a small voice shouts up into the stairwell.

I can see the stairs ever so slightly in the light that seems as if it's fading in and out. I round the corner to see the door open at the bottom of the stairs. A woman holding a torch smiles at me, "Are you hurt?"

I want to cry and tell her I am dead inside, but I don't. I shake my head and stumble down the last couple steps. She backs away so I can leave the stairwell. A man's leg sticks out the bottom, keeping the door ajar.

She points behind her, "I can't seem to get the main door open." Her words are desperate and edgy. I look at the main door in the torchlight and shake my head, "You won't get that one open. We need a window."

She swallows and nods, "Okay. I know where a window is. What section did you come from?"

I point upward.

She sniffles, "I don't understand what's happened. Even the emergency lights have shut off."

"Where is the window?"

She shakes the torch and points to the right.

"You lead the way and I'll break the window." I need to get to Anna. She must be freaking out by now.

We walk through a dark, wide hallway, I can tell we are in the nicer part of the labs, where the general public gets to see everything. God knows what's in the black lab, besides my dead friend and my trapped father.

I can't think about it all, I just can't. The coward in me is strong. She was trained well. She pushes me on, to get me out.

The lady opens a door with no scanners and light floods us both. I see her better now. She's Michael's age and fragile. Her bones would break faster than a chicken's. She has dark hair and dark eyes with a worried look.

The window looks over an alleyway between the buildings at ground level. It's tinted to make it hard to see in. The light of the rising sun is just hitting the buildings.

I walk to the window, examining it. There is no latch to open it. I look at the huge chair to the right. It's an office of sorts. There are metal cabinets and glass desktops with maps underneath. I grab the huge chair and drag it to the window. I lift it up and swing as hard as I can. The window bends almost and then cracks slightly. I swing the chair again, this time I use everything that's left. The window cracks but doesn't fall out. I drag the chair back, pick it up and run at the window with it. The chair almost pushes me back, but the window buckles and the glass falls out, taking the chair with it.

I stand there and breathe as the fresh air hits me.

I don't want the freedom that is there in the fresh air.

I want the man that's dead upstairs and the other one in the basement. I can't face her without them.

The woman has dropped the torch, leaving it to burn the carpet. I almost put it out, but then I remember where I am and what's left.

I follow her out the window, not looking back.

The streets are filled with people. Scared people, who have never lived with the nothingness the rest of us faced. Their city is worthless. It's now no different than any other corner of this world.

I don't know that we made the right choice but I know we made the only one we had. The breeder farms are done, the work camps are for nothing, and the rebellion doesn't matter anymore.

My feet almost slap against the street as I make my way to the apartment we left Anna at. I almost don't recognize the building when I get close to it. In the light it looks magical and not old at all, but she's there on the steps. She's sitting, waiting for me… us.

She sees me, sees the truth instantly. She doesn't jump up. She stays seated on the front steps, avoiding the truth I bring with me.

Her eyes are bright blue, wide and glistening when I get close enough to see them.

I stop, I can't do it. I drop to my knees, in the crowded street with the lost strangers surrounding us both, and sob.

Her slim fingers lift to her face, covering her mouth. We stare at one another, tears streaming our faces. I shake my head subtly. It's the only time I will ever tell her this.

She cries harder.

I look down and let the shame of my failure cloak me in guilt, so heavy I will never be free of it.

I close my eyes and wait for my father to show up, or the infected, or something worse—God only knows what that could be. Instead, her skinny arms wrap around me and hold me. I am not worthy of her love and forgiveness, but I am grateful she is there.

She takes my hand and we start the long walk out of the city. The people we pass are starting to panic; no one has answers. They fear war and starvation. They huddle and fight, and feel all of the things we all felt a decade ago. All of the things they got to avoid because they were apart of the chosen ones. The ones who got to live in the city and be safe.

Anna grips my fingers, almost pulling me along. When we get to the gate, there is no one. We walk along the bridge over the river to the borderlands, not speaking.

"EMMA!"

There it is. There is the man who will not die because I won't let him. He deserves to live. I turn back to see him standing there, wild-eyed and savage.

Anna and I stop walking.

Michael storms towards me, out of breath and crazed looking. He points, "YOU LITTLE BITCH! YOU THINK WE CAN'T REBUILD THIS? YOU THINK THIS IS THE END?"

I can tell by the wild look on his face, it is. He can't rebuild, not this. Not without the power.

"YOU THINK YOU CAN STOP ME? YOU'RE LENNY'S DAUGHTER, THROUGH AND THROUGH! CHICKEN SHIT LENNY!"

I turn away from him, dragging Anna with me. He's trying to get me to kill him and let him off easy.

"DON’T YOU TURN YOUR BACK ON ME!"

But I don’t look back. The world is fair and even, and everyone is the same, including him. I want to kill him but that would spare him the filth and disgusting things I have had to endure to live. I want him to know about the mess he made, the real version. Not the one he's been living.

"EMMAAAAAAA!" His screams become pathetic. He isn’t scary anymore.

I glance at Anna and smile, "I am Lenny's daughter, through and through."

She smiles back through her tears, "Yeah, you are."

Chapter Eight

"I need to know how," she whispers.

I glance at her from my log and sigh, "Why?"

Anna shakes her head, "I just do. We might die out here in the woods, and I don't want to die and not know how."

I take a bite of rabbit and stare at the campfire. My voice is hollow when I speak, "Will was just had no more life support. The machines didn't breathe for him, so he didn't breathe anymore. He just stopped."

I can hear the tears I won't look at, "Did you kiss him goodbye?"

I shake my head, "I couldn't. I just left." I pick at the meat, "Bernie was a gunshot to the back. He was shot once but still managed to send the missile. Then he got shot again."

She sobs silently, except for the sniffles. Sometimes she makes her wheeze.

I don't want anymore to eat, but I know I have to. I'm sick, with myself and the whole circumstance.

I look at her, "We're lost, you know that right?"

She nods, wiping away the tears.

Everywhere we've walked I've whistled for him, but he hasn't come. I'm terrified they didn't make it.

I fall asleep that night next to her on the ground.

I wish I'd dreamt when I wake up; at least then I could have seen his face or listened to him singing that song with the Hey Ho. Instead, I wake to the feel of cool wind on my face. I haven't felt cool wind in a long time. The hot summer feels like it's never going to end, the same way the cold winter does.

I open an eye and see Anna setting some fruit on a leaf for me.

She's used my knife from my boot to cut the apples she has. I grimace. She sneers and whispers harshly, "I washed it."

"It's a cold wind," I mutter as I stand up, stretching my back and picking the ant off of my tank top.

She nods and passes me the broad leaf. I eat an apple slice and savor the flavor. "Where did you find the apples?"

She points. I never noticed in the dark that we're beside a farmhouse. The orchard has been overrun but the fruit trees are covered. My mouth drops, "Wow."

I give her a curious look, "You check out the farmhouse?"

She nods, "Empty." Sometimes she doesn't even say the words, just mouths them. I'm getting better at reading her lips.

She points at a hill to the left, "That's where Bernie's house is."

I look over, "You sure?"

She nods and takes a big bite of apple. "Bernie always said he would go to the farm a few miles over and eat apples. He worried they might be radioactive."

I look at my bite in the apple and grimace.

She shrugs and swallows.

I whistle, hoping he can hear me, as I walk to the farmhouse. It's a beautiful property but the house is a mess. The brown siding is rotting off and the inside looks like it's suffered through an earthquake. The stairs are shifted. It's a perfect place for the animals and infected to hide. I close the crooked front door and don't go in. It's one of the rules I have—don't go in unless there is no other option. At this point, going in is an option only for curiosity's sake.

The trees look amazing; they don't look sick at all. The leaves are bright and green, and the apples are bright and red. They are ready to harvest fast this year.

The dry borderlands are surprisingly good for farming. I pick another apple and walk towards Anna. She's staring off into space, holding her leaf of food, but not moving. Her face is lost in whatever she's remembering. Her eyes drop down as a blush crosses her face but she doesn't smile. I can imagine what she's remembering.

I can imagine the pain she's in.

I know that pain. It's a dusty, dry, hollow ache in my heart too. It's the feel of my lips pressed against his hand. He wasn't normal, or functional, or sane, but he was my match in this crazy world where things don't make sense anyway.

I nod, "Let's start walking towards the hills and see if it's the right way."

My words pull her from the daydream. She gets up, still forcing herself to eat. Our footsteps are the only sound surrounding us, besides the slight whistle of the warm wind through the orchard. The fruit is almost as good as drinking water. The juice it makes in my mouth as I take small bites, quenches some of my thirst.

We are out of water and ammo, and I am out of care. If I drop dead in the dusty hills in front of us, I don't care. I want Leo, Sarah, Jake, and even Star, but I want Will more. I even want Bernie more because I want that look in Anna's eyes to come back. Her face isn't sad; it's the opposite. I can see she's grateful for what she had, even if it was short lived. Her bravery knows no bounds, and I am the only one who is never going to be okay again. She will be. She has been disappointed so much in this life, that even a broken heart can't stop her spirit.

We enter the denser forest, picking up the pace. I have no gun, or bow, or anything. I have my knife.

I don't know what I thought the world looked like; I never gave it much thought. It was all survival before, but now with him gone, it feels like the world is broken. I think I finally know what it feels like to be normal. Everyone else has lived through this all along, but I haven't. I've survived and now I'm not sure I want to.

We hike until my throat dries out and the apples are gone. She sits down on a rock in the middle of nowhere and shakes her head.

I nod, "I know. We're lost." I whistle again and sit down next to her. The forest is silent, not a good sign.

I don’t even want to listen to the sounds of the forest. I just want to close my eyes.

"You have to stop, Em."

I frown at her, "What?"

Tears fill her eyes making them sparkle; they're so blue. Her lip quivers as she shakes her head, "You have to stop. I see it. He wouldn’t want this to end you. I see the anger and will to live are gone. They would want us to find the others and be safe."

She is still the fragile girl standing outside my door with big blue eyes, wanting to sacrifice herself for Jake.

My eyes fill with tears, "I just don’t know how to feel." My voice cracks. "He died for me. He died, but I coulda lived. I coulda lived through that bullet. I'm stronger than he was."

She nods, "I know, but he didn’t want you to get shot." Her voice makes the high moan of the infected when she whispers.

I close my eyes and shudder. The tears are coming faster than I can cry them out. They're choking me up.

A scent hits me as warm fur smothers me and huge paws wrap around me. He found us. I wrap my arms around his neck, digging my fingers into his fur. I feel her arms wrap around us too. He pants into my neck, making his crazy wolf noises. I can't stop shaking.

His smell is the same as always. He nips at me lightly. I nod, "I know. I'm sorry I left you again."

Anna cries into him too. The three of us sit at the top of a hill, weeping and hugging. His head lifts, looking behind us. I swear he's looking for Will and Bernie. His yellow eyes scan the hill and then me. I shake my head, sobbing harder. He puts his head into the wind and cries out the haunting sound he made when Meg died.

I lift my face, letting his song become part of the wind on my skin. He finishes and stands, like he's ready to go home. I am too.

Anna takes my hand, squeezing hard. She smiles, "We'll be okay."

I nod, wiping my face and follow Leo down the hillside. He keeps checking behind his shoulder to make sure we're still there.

He isn't going to trust us for a while.

At the bottom of the hill, I recognize the road we've come upon. He walks, looking around nervously until we reach the entrance to the driveway. My heart lifts a little when we get in view of the house. It looks the same. No cars, no wars, no anger, and no strangers. Just a house, a rock pile grave, and a yard filled with memories I don't want, but I love anyway. I love the fact I can close my eyes and see them all.

Star comes running out. Her eyes look behind us, but she knows when we get closer. Her eyes drop. Her destroyed expression becomes part of the memories I don't want. Jake's face is next. He looks past us. His gaze settles on Anna's face. Whatever the look on her face is, it tells him everything he needs to know. He stops walking, watching her and waiting for her to change the news.

Star does something I don't expect. She wraps her arms around me, "Is he gone?"

I nod once. She shakes, crying silently. "Will too?"

I nod again, hugging her back.

Jake sees us, his blue eyes glisten with the tears filling them. He shakes his head, "No way. No way. We just got him back. No, he's strong. You wait and see, he's gonna come." The tears leave his eyes, streaming down his face. Leo walks to him, rubbing against him.

Jack's son comes out of the house. His face falls. He presses his lips together and lowers his gaze. Sarah bursts from the house, leaping at me. I hug her and Star.

"You made it back." She looks past me, "Where's Will and Bernie?"

I shake my head, letting her down on the grass. Her little face loses the joy she had. She starts to cry silently, turning away from me. She walks to Meg's grave. Leo follows her, as does Andy when he comes walking out of the house. They sit next to the rock pile with their backs to us. Andy holds her hand. Somehow, it's the worst and best thing I've ever seen. Even Leo doesn't mind Andy anymore.

Jake and Anna are sobbing, holding each other.

Star wipes her face, "How?"

I sniffle, "Bernie got shot by a guard in the city and I killed Will."

Jake looks at me but Anna shakes her head. She points at me, "He would have wanted that choice. You made it fair for everyone."

Jake shakes his head, "What?"

"Marshall knew about a missile in the city that could be launched, and it would take away all the power from the whole country. No trucks, cars, and technology. No city and breeder farms or work camps. No one doing better than anyone else. Me and Bernie found it, and with his last breath, he launched the missile. Will was on a machine that kept him alive, when the power went out... so did Will." I realize how cold it sounds as I say it.

No one says anything for a minute.

Finally, Star nods, "I'm glad Bernie got to fix his mistakes. It's always bothered him that he was part of it."

Jack's son points at the house, "We noticed the power was gone. Nothing is working."

Jake wipes his eyes, "Will would have done the same thing. He wanted this to end, always."

I shake my head. I don't have anything to add to it. I don't want to talk about it. I turn and walk to Sarah and Leo. I sit on my knees next to her. She looks at me with a tear-stained face. She sniffles, "I was just telling Meg to go find Bernie and Will and make sure they stay with her, so we can all find them again."

Her words are like a knife in my heart.

I stare at the grave, "She'll keep them entertained and busy until we get there."

Leo lays down and we sit in silence, grieving the same people for different reasons.

Chapter Nine

"Ten more people, Em. We can't keep this up."

I look at Sully, Jack's son, and shake my head, "What can we do? It's only two months till the snow hits. We can't turn people away."

He sighs, "Em, the entire camp is on its way. Jack told me how big that camp was. The place they go for winter has been taken over by other people."

In the last two months, the changes that have taken place have made everything harder for everyone. Everyone but us rebels, who were used to being cut off.

I shake my head, "We need to help them set up their camp here. How many houses are built?"

He shrugs, "Four."

I nod, "The barn can convert if it's needed. We need to make sure the fireplaces are set up."

He nods, "I know. I just wanted to tell you, ten more people have arrived, with word that a lot more are on their way."

"Great." I leave the kitchen, walking past people straggling in. I grab an apple and some seeds from the sunflowers, and go look for Anna.

She's still green around the gills and looking exhausted but she doesn't stop. She points at the barn and tells the man with the armload of fire wood where it needs to go.

She smiles when she sees me. There is joy on her face; that is one of the few things keeping me going. I pass her the apple, "You have to eat."

She sighs, "Em, I ate like an hour ago."

I shake my head, "You eat this and I won't bug you for a couple hours."

Sarah stumbles over, running with Leo. Her face is lit up, "The meat racks work!"

I smile at her, "Did it dry them?"

She nods, "Just like the ones at the retreat."

Jake strolls over, bringing food and water. Anna gives him a look, "I'm fine!"

He gives me a curious look. I nod, "She seems good. She's only two-and-a-half-months pregnant."

He scoffs, "She's seventeen."

Anna points at him. He puts his hands in the air, "Fine."

Sarah rubs her belly, "I'm excited. I can't wait for the baby."

I sigh, "I can't wait until Star finishes getting the solar panels hooked up again. A hot shower is going to be bliss."

Jake nods, "A shower and a flushing toilet."

Anna shakes her head, "I still think we need to go ahead with our plan. I don’t want to be here with all these people."

Sarah frowns, "We can't leave Meg here." Anna nods, "I know, honey, but this place is getting too packed. It's going to become the retreat all over again."

Sarah doesn’t see what was wrong at the retreat. She doesn’t know about the things that were going on behind the scenes. Hell, I barely knew about them. Sarah likes the mansion. She likes having Andy with her, and of course Leo. They spend their time running around the yard. He still favors his leg but he's much better than before.

I glance around at the activity going on. Star is shouting at the people, leading them and directing them. People are carrying wood and dragging poles to build another log house and the barn has been converted into a metal working shop. Jake calls it the smithy; it makes me laugh.

Sully walks out of the house and I catch a glimpse and a smile from Star. Jake leans in to me, "They think they're being so sneaky."

I can't help but love seeing people happy and in love. It makes everything else seem less—less important and scary. I glance at Jake and wish I could see him the way I did before I met Will. Will who took up all the space in my heart.

"Don't you wish we could all just have a 'happy ever after'?" Jake and I look at Anna. We don't say anything. She rubs her belly, "I wish every day Bern coulda known I was pregnant."

Jake sighs and walks off.

I shake my head, "Don't pay attention to him."

She laughs bitterly, "Bernie would have had the same opinion of us being pregnant. He didn't even want to have sex with me. He was such a stickler about the age thing—and the Will and Jake being massive thing."

I laugh with her but I'm scared of her having a baby. We barely got through Jake having a cut on his leg and Leo having a bullet wound.

I watch her face change a little and know she's scared too. She gives me an odd look, "Can we just go to the farmhouse? I have this funny feeling we should go there."

I nod, "Yeah. We need to help them decide on a leader. People need a leader."

Her eyes dart at Star, "Star and Sully should stay here and run this. It could be a work farm, just a free one."

I bite my lip and think on it. It makes sense to let them stay here and me, Sarah, Jake, and Anna go to the farmhouse. We wouldn't overburden the well or the small farmhouse. The fields are ready to be planted again and the farm here has the seed from the camps. We could do it, but the idea of being alone with just the few of us makes me nervous.

Me and Leo alone is nothing but adding them means responsibility.

Against my instincts I nod, "Okay. I'll talk to Star." I turn away and walk to where she's shouting at the crowds. She points at the barn, "All scrap metal in the barn!" She turns and smirks at me, "What am I doing wrong?"

I laugh, "Nothing. I just wanted to ask you something."

She searches my eyes for a second, "What?"

"Would you want to stay here and help them run it or would you rather come with me, Anna, Jake, and Sarah to the farmhouse?"

She scowls, "We just got this place to the way we want it. We have enough people to turn it into a functioning farm, and the solar shit that was stored in the metal bunker is almost done being hooked up. We'll have power in no time."

I nod, "Anna wants to go. I think she's scared of having the baby here with all these people." I glance around discretely.

Star folds her arms, "I guess I can understand that." She looks at everything and then back at me, "But I want to stay. I'm not Star the massage lady, or Star, Marshall's bitch. I like this. I like being me here. Me and Sully can stay but when that baby is born y'all better send word."

I roll my eyes, "It's one day of walking."

She scoffs, "We'll have vehicles up and running by then. The diesel vehicles might be salvageable."

I wince, "Keep that information under wraps. We don't want everyone to know that."

Her eyes harden, "You should have killed him, Em."

I nod, "I know."

The hard look becomes a sparkle, "Maybe we'll get the chance again."

I laugh, "Maybe. We're gonna head out tomorrow."

She nods, "Okay."

I smirk, "Andy is gonna stay."

She shakes her head, "Screw that."

I nod towards a lady with dark-blonde hair. She's standing in the middle of the yard, holding his little hand and brushing his hair from his eyes.

Star sees it and nods, "I think her baby was one of the ones Marshall took."

I shudder, "He was a sick bastard."

She nods, "Maybe we'll get a chance to kill them too."

I'm sure we look the same as we watch the lady and dream about murdering the baby killers. I still owe that to Meg. I know I abandoned it, but I still remember owing her.

We leave the next day at sunrise. We don’t have much with us; we look like we're going hiking. Star agreed to keep the whole thing quiet for us. Anna had been in the breeder farms and people have strange notions about the breeder babies still. Some of them still believe the propaganda Marshall fed them. Others have seen the ones from the city, the ones our father was experimenting on. The ones he let do whatever they wanted to. I still don’t understand that, letting the city people live in fear of them. Nothing makes sense about my father and the UN story. I wish sometimes I'd tortured answers from him, instead of walking away, but I think maybe he might have felt like I cared about him if I'd wondered. I don’t care about him. I hate that Lenny believed my mother had cheated on him and got pregnant, but I loved that Lenny never let me know I wasn’t his. He kept me alive, the daughter of the enemy, the man who killed the world.

I refuse to be anything but Lenny's daughter. Sarah looks back as we leave the driveway, "We shoulda brought Andy."

I shake my head, "That lady needs him more than we do. We'll be busy enough with the new baby."

"I guess. I just hope he doesn't forget me." She looks at Leo and walks ahead with him.

Anna nudges me, "She'll be okay."

Jake shakes his head, "She's right. We shot his mom right in front of him; now we're leaving him with some random lady? That's cold. We owe that kid at least our protection."

I don't look at him, I can't. I can't own what I did there. I can't regret it.

Anna whispers harshly, "She killed Meg, maybe she never pulled the trigger but she got them captured. Screw her. She deserved to die."

Jake gives her a mean stare, "You sound like her." He nudges towards me.

Anna flashes a crazed look, "Good. Thank you."

He shakes his head, looking meaner than ever, "It wasn't a compliment." He stalks off with Sarah and Leo.

Anna looks at me, "He's sounding more like Will."

I nod and choke down the pain that name brings me.

We walk for a long time without breaking or talking. When we get to the old freeway, me and Leo break off ahead. We run silently and scout. Nothing moves. Somewhere on this stretch of broken road, Lenny's remains lay. I push that thought away and look around for movement.

A high-pitch scream fills the air. I wish I had my bow; a gun will bring more of them. Sarah isn't immune. We should have grabbed more vaccines from the city before we ruined it. We should have done many things before we ruined it, like save Will and kill my father, before he killed Bernie.

I regret everything.

The high moan comes again. I look back at Jake and Anna and point at the tree to the side of the road. They start climbing. Leo crouches low, giving me a look. I nod and move hunched over, pulling the handguns I took from the weapons stash, from my leg holsters. I listen for the moans, but I hear something else. Leo's ears twitch.

We crawl amongst the old, grown-over wreckage and both stop instantly when we see it.

Horses and men are fighting the infected but not killing them. They're putting them in a cart with a cage on it. The horses are huge, a type of horse I've never seen before. They're shaggy and massive. I don’t really know what to assume about what I'm seeing, but even Leo is stopped, looking stunned. We sit behind an old shell of a truck and watch down the highway, as they get them into the cart and then mount the horses.

They ride, pulling them through the wreckage, away from us. I stay there, crouched and confused for a while. Leo sits and yawns, and I know the danger is gone, but it doesn’t make sense.

I wave at Anna. She brings Sarah and Jake.

"What was it?"

I shake my head, "I don’t know. It was horses with a cart and cage, and men taking the infected alive."

Jake wrinkles his nose, "Maybe they're still trying to find a cure."

I shake my head, "I don’t know." It seems weird. We cross into the forest on the other side of the freeway and make the run I made ten years ago.

It takes us all day to get there, but as we emerge from the woods, we all stop when we see it.

Anna looks at me, "People from the camps?"

I shake my head, not breaking my stare from the cabin with the lights on. Candles must be lit inside making the windows glow. I can see smoke from a fire outside in the yard, between the barn and the house. My heart sinks. My spare bow and quiver are in the barn bunker.

"We can camp here for tonight and then make our way back tomorrow."

Anna gasps, "Em, we came all this way and this house is ours."

She has become me in a lot of ways, and somehow, I've become Will. I don't want to kill the people in the house for it. They got there before us.

Jake shakes his head, "Em is right. We leave for the mansion tomorrow."

Sarah moans, "My feet hurt and I don't want to go all the way back. I don't want to sleep outside."

She's tired and whiny. Jake wraps an arm around her, "Sarah, those people got their first, they don't deserve to die for finding an empty farmhouse."

Sarah moans and sits on a log. I sit beside her and nudge her, "I'm tired too."

In the dim light of the moon, I can see her pouting. It makes me smile. She wrinkles her nose at me and shakes her head.

Anna opens a sack she brought and passes us all some dried meat and apples. We drink the last of our water in silence, wishing we were inside of that house.

I rip off some dried meat for Leo, but I don't see him. I whistle softly but he's not there.

"Must be hunting or doing his circle," I mutter, but I don't feel like that's the case. I feel weird about him not being there.

Jake sits next to me on the log, shifting where it sits suspended. He looks down, "Wanna have a fire?"

I nod, "Yeah. They can't get mad if we have a fire. We aren't doing anything wrong being here. We aren't too close to the house."

He sighs and rubs his eyes, "Come help me get wood."

I almost mock him, but I know he's been trying harder. He's trying to not be the grasshopper who played all summer. He gets up and grabs my hand in his. The touch tugs at my heart. He pulls me up and into the woods.

I don't jerk my hand free; I like the touch. It doesn't mean the same thing to me that it does for him. Anna was right, being around them more has helped me be around them, and not be in love with every guy our age that I see. I'm accustomed to them now.

We crunch through the forest, looking for wood. He looks back, "What do you think about Anna having a baby? Really think?"

"I think it's good. She has a piece of Bernie that's hers. He will be there forever in the form of that baby."

He scoffs, "She's seventeen. She's going to fall in love again. She probably wasn't in love. She's too young."

"Jake, she loved him. She isn't a normal seventeen-year old. She's way older and she's seen way more. Bernie loved her too. He hated that she was so young and he hated that he loved her, but he did. I don't think she'll ever love again. I think she'll be a good mom. Sometimes she's crazy, but she's going to be a good mom."

He breaks the branches as we walk past them, "I guess."

I smile. He still does it, even though we can find our way back easily.

I pick up a piece of wood but he takes it. "Will you ever get over Will?"

I shake my head, "I don't know. Will you?"

He shakes his head, "No. I get why he became the mean asshole he did. I get the pain and sorrow he'd seen made him who he was."

"I noticed the happy, sweet Jake has been gone. I'm sorry."

He takes the wood from my hands that I grab, "It's not your fault. Will chose saving you over himself. That's the kind of person he was. Even before, that's the kind of guy he was."

"Tell me something you remember from before."

His voice breaks ever so slightly, "My mom used to take us out to movies. She loved the air conditioning in the summer. She would drag us to the movie and make us watch whatever crap Anna could watch. Me and Will would complain and complain. So finally one day, we were in the city for the movie and Will convinces her we can go to a show by ourselves. Anna was like three and they were going to see the Smurfs. Will got her to let us go see the newest Paranormal Activity movie. She let us go; scared the heck out of me. I hate scary movies but Will loved it. I pretended to love it too, but he could tell I was scared. So when we got home, he let me crash in his room with him until I wasn't scared anymore. He slept on the floor and let me sleep on the bed, but never told mom or anyone."

His arms are full from the wood I've stacked in them and we're far from Anna and Sarah, but I don't want to stop listening to him talk.

He turns around and smiles, "He let me pick next time. I chose the newest Batman."

I smile.

He starts walking back to Anna and Sarah, looking at his broken branches.

My heart stops when I hear screaming. Jake looks at me, "What was that?"

I shake my head, listening better. The scream happens again. It's my name being screamed. I break into a run, leading Jake and me to the farmhouse. I know the way and that's where the screaming is coming from.

In the firelight across the field, I can see movement but I can't make it out. Jake is keeping up with me, I can hear his footsteps landing hard. I run silently, as always. I slip against the barn, hearing the cries of Sarah and the high moan of Anna. What if they think she's infected. I pull my guns and sneak around the far side of the barn.

I see Sarah and Anna's legs on the ground with a huge man's. Sarah is crying so hard I can barely make it out, but I do. She cries, "WILL!"

I drop to my knees, frozen. My guns clunk to the hard dry ground.

Jake launches himself at the heap of hugging and wrestling people.

My stunned and silent face doesn't want to react, in case it's wrong. I don't swallow or breathe or cry. I sit frozen as Will gets off of Anna and Sarah and turns to smile at Jake. Jake lifts him right off the ground, hugging him mid-air.

Leo is jumping up, licking and nipping at Will. I don't think I've ever seen him so excited, but I have no response. I don't have excitement or passion. I think I'm angry, maybe at myself or the trickery going on in front of my face.

"Jakey! Jakey!" Will's voice cracks. He doesn't sound normal but he says Jakey like before. I hate that name.

He puts Will down and slaps him hard on the arm, "How, man? How the hell did you get here?"

He shakes his head; he can't speak. He coughs and turns to face me.

Our eyes meet, and for a second I believe it's him, but I know I touched his dead hand. I shake my head; it must be a trick of my father's.

Will walks to me, silencing the others except for the sniffles and tears.

Will drops to his knees in front of me. He runs a hand across my cheek. I close my eyes and shake my head, "It can't be you."

He leans in, smelling exactly like him and presses his lips against my forehead, "It's me, baby."

Tears stream my cheeks, "I felt you. You were dead."

He shakes his head, "I was awake when you and Bernie came in the room. Whatever he gave me, woke me up. I felt you holding my arm and Bernie sticking me with a huge needle. When they realized I was awake, they sounded the alarms to catch Bernie. They figured he was bad. Some guy with a bullet wound to the chest was brought in on a stretcher, and I was taken to a different area so they could try to work on him. They brought me down a couple floors. I was left with the guards until the lights went out. They left us there, but the medical staff got us out when the fire got bad."

I mutter blankly, "The fire. The lady with the torch."

He looks confused, "I don't know who that was, but there was a fire and the whole city is burning now. I got away in the chaos. I couldn't find my way to Bernie's, so I came here. I knew eventually, you would come here." He kisses the side of my face, "You always come back here."

I lift my hands up and drag them over his face. "It's you?" The man on the stretcher wasn't Will.

He nods and kisses my palm. I collapse into him, wrapping around him completely. "I left you, I'm so sorry I left you. I thought he was you. I'm so sorry."

He coughs funny when I squeeze him and laughs, "Easy, Em. My lung is still weak." He pulls back my head and shakes his, "You made it out of the city. That's what matters."

I shake my head but Jake slaps him on the back, "I told you, nothing can kill this cantankerous old bastard."

Will laughs and hugs me again.

Instantly, we are surrounded by arms and breath. Anna is wheeze talking so fast none of us can catch it, but we can feel the joy in her shaking body. I close my eyes and hold on. I don't know if we'll stay this way. I don't even care. He's alive right now. My heart is angry for believing him dead, for leaving him to die in that building, for kissing the hand of a stranger goodbye and giving up.

I haven't changed so much. I am still the girl who turns her back on the dying to save her own skin.

Chapter Ten

Me and Leo take the first watch in the barn.

I have the rifle and my bow from the bunker, and the handguns from the gun storage at Bernie's.

In one of the windows of the farmhouse, I see Anna walk across the kitchen. It's dark inside and out; nothing moves except her and the wheat blowing in the field. She slips across the gravel driveway, almost completely silent. I hear the familiar creak of the boards on the stairs.

She creeps across the hay and sits next to me. I don't look at her. I keep my eye on the fields.

"Is it possible Bernie made it too?"

I close my eyes and recall the way he slumped over the keyboard as he gave out his last breath. I had to expect she would ask it though. I would have asked it. I would have gone back. I never would have taken her word that he was dead.

She must hate me for lying about Will and doubt me about Bernie.

I shake my head, "Anna, if he's alive then my father performed a miracle, because minutes after he was shot twice at point blank, the power went out. About an hour later, a lady lit the building he was in on fire."

She starts to cry quietly, "I can't do it without him."

My lip creeps out as tears slip down my cheeks. I have nothing to offer her. I ran up the stairs and turned my back on him after he saved us all. My cowardice is shameful.

I speak softly, "I would do it all differently now. I would have let

Marshall take me in, so he could have set the missiles and destroyed everything. You, Bernie, Meg, Jake, Sarah, Will, Star, and Sully would be safe."

She sighs and lays back in the hay, "Em, you laid with the dead to help me escape. You saved Meg, Me, Sarah, and Jake. You helped Bernie stop the bad people having power over us all. You are the fiery crow, even when you don't try to be."

I scoff, "Some fiery crow I turned out to be." I glance back at her, "I think Bernie was the crow. He let the man he used to be die, so he could be a new man for you. A man you could be proud of and tell your baby about."

She smiles and wipes her eyes, "Thanks, Em."

I shake my head, "Don't thank me. I never brought him home."

Leo moves to lay with her. She runs her fingers through his downy fur. "Why do you think they were rounding up the infected?"

I watch the field and listen to the rest of the world, "I don't know."

"I think it's your dad, I think he's got an evil plan."

I nod, watching the darkness, "He always seems to have one."

"Why didn't you kill him?"

I shake my head, "I wanted him to see how it really was here. He's been living in that city with all those Gen babies of his scaring everyone into being under his thumb. He never had an army or anything, beyond the guards. He had all those Gen kids. Everyone was so scared and timid there, they just let him do everything the way he wanted. No one challenged him I bet." I look back at her, "Bernie stopped that and made it so he has to see how we have lived. Think of how last winter was for you. Alone with Jake in the woods, freezing and starving. My dad was in the city, nice and warm and torturing people."

She presses her lips together, "We hid out in a house and burned the furniture to stay warm. Then the snow was melting and we saw you and this guy here. He came up, growling and acting all mean, but I gave him a piece of rabbit. He ate it and then we became friends."

I nod, "Little traitor. I figured there was something. There was no way he was just so easy around you from the start." I smirk back, "I'm gad though. For everything that's gone wrong, the things that went right have changed my life."

She kicks me, "Gimme my rifle and go see my brother. I think he's sort of bummed out that you're hiding up here, instead of with him." She rolls her eyes, "Lord knows he's gonna come up here if you don't, and then we'll all get murdered while you two mess up the watch."

I think for a second and then pass her the rifle. It's hers anyway.

She gets into position with Leo, shoving me out of the way.

"You should be sleeping, you're pregnant."

She shrugs, "I can sleep tomorrow." She looks up at the stars and smiles, "I miss him tonight and I can't sleep, so I'd rather sit here under the stars and see if I can guess which one is him."

She is killing me.

I get up and walk down to the house. I creep inside to the room in the back where I know he's sleeping. I open the door softly and step inside. My stomach is in knots, but I want to touch him.

I pull off my pants, shirt, and boots, crawling into the bed in my underwear and tank top. He pulls back the covers, "I was getting hurt feelings."

I laugh as quietly as I can, "I just don't think it's hit me that you're here. I don't trust it. Everything else is wrecked—why do I get to be the one who gets lucky and finds the man she loves?"

He leans on his arm in the moonlight and grins a shitty smile at me, "I knew you loved me." He reaches out, taking my hand in his. I close my eyes and remember how it felt in the lab room. In the dark I would swear it was him, but now in the dark of this room, I can feel the calluses from picking at a guitar. The hand in the room never had that. He pulls me into his arms, whispering into my cheek, "Emma, you and me deserve all the luck we can get. If it's one day's worth, or it's two years' worth, or it's a whole lifetime, we deserve it. After everything we've been through, we deserve every second." He kisses against the edge of my lips, "I love you with my whole heart and I'll never lie to you again."

I nod into his face, pushing into the kiss and let him pull me under his body.

When I wake up in the morning, he's gone but Leo is crashed on the bed with me. He lifts his face, making his wolf smile and yawns.

I rub his fur and decide we need to stay in this room a little longer. Bad things rarely happen when I'm in bed; it's mostly when I get up and start the day.

I give Leo a deep rub down. He rolls onto his back so I get the parts he loves the most. His belly and armpits are his favorite. I scratch and he starts to make his wolf purring noise. Sarah comes in with a plate of food and crawls into the bed with us. I steal some of the pancake on her plate. It's slathered in apple butter. She gives Leo a piece and smiles, "Can we just stay in one place, all of us?"

I nod, "I think so. Unless you have somewhere you need to be?" My Granny used to say that to my dad all the time. He always had somewhere else to be. It wasn't that he didn't want to be with me; it was that he wanted to be ready.

Sarah takes another bite of pancake. It was the one thing she had to take from Bernie's, the pancake mix. I'm glad now she did.

"Will made them."

I smile, "You glad he's back?"

She nods, "Yeah. I just hope Bernie can find his way too."

I frown, "Honey, Bernie is gone. I watched him die."

She shakes her little head, "Emma, you were wrong about Will;

you're probably wrong about Bernie too."

The pancake tastes funny to me and hard to swallow. I get it down and nod, "Yeah, I hope so."

Jake comes in and flops onto the bed too. He smirks, "How ya doing?"

I give Sarah a smile, "Can you get me some water?"

She jumps up, taking Leo with her. I give Jake a look, "I'm waiting for something terrible to happen. It feels like we should be on the move and killing or fighting. I just don't trust any of this."

He gives me a grim look, "I feel the same, like something bad is coming."

I shrug and lay back down, letting him lie across my legs, "Guess we wait and see, huh?"

He slaps my leg, "Actually, something maybe not awesome has come."

I give him a look, "Huh?"

His grin splits into the goofy one I love, "The cooking circle ladies are here. They just arrived from Marshall's camp. They brought food and seeds, and hands to help us get this place functional for winter."

I smile back, "Really?" Something about the numbers increasing is making me happier. Older ladies who might be able to deliver a baby also make me happy.

He nods, "Yup. Will's out there chatting with them now. They brought all the seeds they've harvested, and because this place is between the retreat and the trade towns, they're going to use it as their winter base and summer farming area."

I sigh a type of relief, I swear, I have never felt before.

"I know, I almost sounded exactly the same when I saw them coming."

I point at him from my back, "You need to get the firewood piles going."

He laughs, "You and Will are soul mates, I swear it. I came in here to avoid the firewood."

I smack whatever is closest to me, "No, go slacker."

He grabs my hand and lifts me off the bed, dragging me down the hallway. Anna walks past me, looking green again. She points at the bed, "Sleepy."

Jake and I nod. She has been like that for a month.

I see Will in the yard from the kitchen window. He smiles at me but keeps talking to the ladies, "If we have that many more people, we need to start getting ready. This house only holds so many. We need guards in the trees and to start getting the field ready to prepare for a spring plant. It's gonna need to be tilled so we can use it in the spring. I think we can get a lot accomplished in the two months before the snow hits."

The circle ladies smile at me, waving, "Emma!"

I wave back, "Hi!"

"So this is your place?" The lady with the red tongue on her tee shirt asks. I shake my head, "It's everyone's."

She smirks, "Same old Emma. How's Marshall?" Her eyes gleam.

I cock an eyebrow, "Dead."

She slaps me on the back when I get closer, "That's my girl. I always knew you had it in you. That man was a bastard." I look past them to see the Jake dog running for me. I drop to my knees and he jumps me, slathering me in wet dog kisses.

"Jake dog!"

Jake shoves me, "Shut up."

I rub his face and kiss the top of his shiny head, "Look how chunky you are getting."

The ladies chuckle, "Oh, he never strays too far from the cook pot."

I snort and rub his furry, fat tummy, "I can see that." I glance at Will, "What do you need me to do?"

He doesn't skip a beat, like he's been planning it, "Make arrows and teach a few guys how to make bows and arrows. We'll need them. The ammo is running low. They need to know how to make them and shoot them."

I nod, "Okay." When I stand up, he passes me a hatchet and brushes his lips against mine. It's like we steal a second and the world stops for us. I blush, thinking about the night before, when we break our kiss. I look down and head across the field to the group of men. The snickers of the ladies and Jake make the blush worse, but the fearful look in the eyes of the group of men makes me feel better.

"Who wants to learn how to use a bow and arrow?" I almost dare them with my tone.

They look scared for a second but then nods start coming my way.

I point at the willow tree next to the river on the far side of the field, "We go this way then."

Chapter Eleven

It's my turn in the north tree. Leo is camped at the base of the tree, sleeping. My butt is asleep from sitting for hours, but it makes me feel like, in my small way, it's not easy.

I don't want us to ever take anything for granted again. We need things to not be easy. It made us lazy targets once; we can't ever let that go.

Leo stretches and rolls on his other side. I notice now that the weather is getting colder, he can't lay for very long on the side where the bullet went in.

The crisp of the air is refreshing after the long and smothering heat of the summer. The smell of the fire from the barn where they're fitting shoes on the horses, makes me anxious for winter. Winter in this world is peace. The calm of the snow is the only time I ever really relax. No one can travel in the cold anymore, not that they ever really did. Winter has always been quiet. We work like the ants to make the winter relaxing. Then we hibernate. Me and Leo have never shared a winter with anyone, but somehow I don't think I can remember how it feels to not have them all there. To not belong. I see myself as part of them, no longer on the outside looking in. Maybe it's because they're in my territory now. This was my house and I invited them in.

The log houses are built, to get us by for the winter. They'll be improved upon in the spring, but seeing the little village we have built makes me happy. A crunch in the dry leaves below breaks my daydream. My tree moves as Jake climbs up into it with me. He sits on the branch next to me, giving me a funny look.

"What?"

He shakes his head, "Nan asked me to come and tell you it's time to get ready to go to Bern… Star's."

We try not to say his name too much. It makes Anna crabby, even when she's busy pretending she wants to talk about him. I nod, "Okay. So it's me and you then, huh?"

He sighs, "I guess so. Will is staying, his cough is worse, I swear."

I look out at the woods and the sleeping wolf, "At night when he's sleeping, I swear I can hear something in there. Like he's not fixed. He's struggling for air and his chest sounds like it's crushing him. He can't do much, physically."

His blue eyes meet mine, "Nan said that it might be smart to get some antibiotics."

I flinch, "We took away the power. I don't think they can make it without the power. The lady at the town who sold it to me for you, she said she got it from the farms, from her son.

He nods, "Then we do our best to make sure he stays strong."

I sling my bow over my shoulder and start down the tree, "We need to make sure he understands that too. The colder it's getting, the worse he's getting."

Leo stands and stretches when I get to the bottom. He nudges against me as I look around once more. His perky ears and happy wolf face are exactly how I like to see him. That and the song of the forest make me relax as Jake gets out of the tree. When we leave the woods and start up the field to the house, I nudge Jake, "The book you found on old, horse-drawn carts was a good score."

He smiles, "It worked well. Those horses of Sully's are making plowing the field so much easier."

I smile up at him, "I'm proud of you."

He beams, "Awww shucks, Sis. You're making me blush." But he doesn't blush, I do. It's the first time he's said Sis to me. It's the first time we openly admit there is nothing in us but family love. I look down and walk, but he hits me in the arm lightly, "Yeah, I said Sis. You and Will are the same kind of crazy. Besides, some of the girls who came down from the retreat last month are hot."

I shake my head, fighting my smile, "You should go for that girl Andrea. She's good at this life. She hunts and fishes, cooks, sews, and knows first aid."

He snorts, "You had me at hunts. I still can't gut things. It makes me sick."

Rod, one of the guys from the retreat who is friends with Will, passes us on the field. He carries a bow and quiver. He winks at me. I smile, "Have a good night."

He puts a hand up and walks past us.

I give Jake a frown, "If you don't want to gut, I can show you how to get the meat without gutting them. Jack showed me how."

He nods and holds the door for me when we get to the house, "Sounds good."

I hear the cough from across the house. I walk down the hall to the back room we have claimed as ours. Will is changing his shirt. I can see the sweat on the one he pulls off.

He smiles when he sees me, but I don't smile at him. His scar is fading on his chest. I reach out, touching a fingertip to the line on his chest.

"How was watch?"

I nod, "Boring." He pulls me into his sweaty body. It's cool sweat, not fever like Jake had. I put my hands on his chest, "You have to slow down, Will. You're healing and your lung is still weak." I know how serious my gaze gets; I can feel it. He tries to smile, but I put my finger on the tip of his nose like Granny always did, "You listening to me? You have to slow down. I can't do that again. You can't leave me."

He flashes me the smile that melts everything, "Never again." He kisses my lips softly, "But for the record, I took a bullet to save you."

I shake my head against the stubble on his face, "I would have lived. Next time you let them shoot me. I can live through anything." I don’t say the thing I can't live without. I don’t want to talk about it.

He wraps his arms around me, "You going to see Sully and Star?" I nod. He kisses again, murmuring into my cheek, "You could stay and someone else could go."

I smile, "I can't let Jake go without me."

His smile tightens, "Jake could stay. I don’t want him out there anyway."

I laugh, "He's amazing on the horses. Him and Anna both are great with the horses. I have to go. Can you just rest... for me?"

He nods, tilting my chin up, "I love you."

"I love you too."

He kisses the tip of my nose and steps back, "I'm going to tell Nan that you'll be resting until I get back tomorrow."

He rolls his eyes, "Don’t get Nan involved. That woman is a savage."

I step back again, "That’s the point." I wave, "Leo is going to want to come. He's still not letting me out of his sight, so you have the bed to yourself."

He gives me a sad face; it makes me laugh.

"Behave yourself."

I head down the hall. Jake is laughing, leaning on the counter with Andrea and Kim. He's batting those massive black lashes and chewing a piece of dried meat. Kim blushes and shakes her head.

I walk past him, "You ready?"

He jumps up, "Let's do this. Ladies, it was lovely seeing you all, but I gotta go wrangle some horses. So we can continue this conversation when I get back."

I shake my head at the giggles in the kitchen. His charming antics are impossible to resist. I've been on the receiving end of that smile. I'm just grateful he stopped giving it to me.

Nan nods at me from the cook pit. She points at Jake, "Behave."

He walks with a serious amount of swagger, "Yes, ma'am."

Anna smiles at me from the meat racks. Her nausea ended a few weeks ago, making her able to work with food again, and able to eat things other than just fruit.

"See you tomorrow."

She nods.

Jake points at her, "Make Will relax. He's sounding rough."

She nods again. We walk to the animal barn that was built from the pen the farm already had. Two horses are already saddled. I grin back at Anna, "Thanks."

She waves.

"She looks better."

Jake grunts. He still hasn't come to terms with the baby or the fact Anna had sex; Will is worse.

I get onto the horse and sigh, "My butt's sore and we haven't even started."

He chuckles, "We'll ride fast, I swear." He hops on and steers his horse to the gate. One of the girls with a sweet smile, and an eye on Jake, gets the gate. He winks at her as he rides out. I nearly roll my eyes but they're getting sore from it.

We take off across the field. Leo stays with us the whole ride down the hill to the roadway. I have my handguns holstered on my legs, and my bow and quiver slung over my back. Jake has the sack of water and food in his saddlebags. Sully and Star took hunting parties up into the woods to the spot the cabins had been, where Sully lived before. They raided everything from there, horses, saddlebags, supplies—everything.

The five-hour horse ride is considerably better than walking the whole thing.

Jake and I have done the ride twice. Will can't ride a horse for very long, his chest hurts so Jake and I have to be the ones to do it. We know the way and Star's people know us.

When we cross the planes where we were once taken captive by Fish and Sully, I can't help but feel like it was a hundred years ago. I don't know what changed me more, Will and Bernie dying, walking away from my father, or destroying everything they made. The combination is brutal and I hardly recognize myself.

We see a herd of animals that look like elk. I point at them as we ride. Jake shakes his head, "We don't have time."

I pull an arrow, squeezing my horse between my thighs tighter, and try to pull the arrow back. The horse galloping and the moving animal make it impossible. I don't know how the American Indians did it.

I put the arrow away and catch back up to Jake. My riding is still sloppy and I end up with sores. He rides like he was born to—him, Star and Anna.

We get to the crater that Star showed us before. Jake stops the horse to look. He always does when we reach the crater. I think he will always miss the world the way it was before. He rubs his hand down the horse's face and gives it a nudge. The horse starts again.

When we get to Star's, the guards wave us in.

The mansion and grounds have become a small town. I jump down off the horse and lead it to the barn. A lady comes out and grabs the reigns, "Hey, Emma!"

I smile. I don't know her name, but I know she was in the breeder farms.

Andy comes running up waving his chubby hands at me, "Where's Sarah?"

I wince, "Hey buddy, she's still at the farm. She's helping Anna with racking meat."

He hugs my leg. Jake saves me by pointing out the animals in the pens, "What's that Andy?" Andy giggles and takes his hand to show him something called a cheep.

Star comes up with a grin and muscles like I'm sure I've never seen on a girl. I point, "What is that?"

She laughs, "Been learning to be a smithy." She wraps her arms around me, hugging me fiercely. She pulls back, "How's the farmhouse?"

She means how's Will, but she won't ask. I appreciate that. I nod, "Good. Everyone is good." I point behind me, "I'm going to say hi to Meg."

She winks, "Say hi to Bernie while you're there. It's his bush too."

I turn and walk toward the massive rose bush.

A man walks up to me, meeting me along the way, "Emma!"

I smile when I see him, "Mitch!"

He wraps his arms around me, smelling my hair and shaking his head, "I heard about Will and Bernie. I'm so sorry."

I pull back, "Will's okay."

His face drops, "He's alive?"

I nod.

He sighs, "Oh thank God. I heard he was killed. I nearly died myself."

"He's at the farmhouse I used to hide at. We built a wheat farm there. Got a lot of the retreat people there for the winters."

His smile is still sweet. He nudges me, "You're taking me with you when you go."

I shake my head, "No way. You gotta stay here and help out."

He rolls his eyes, "It's already bigger than it needs to be. Star is figuring out how to make bullets now. She'll have a factory in no time." He stares at her for a second, like he's getting lost in thought and repressed emotions. When he snaps out of it, he shakes his head, "No, I need to leave here."

I understand and nod, "Alright. We ride out tomorrow. Sully wants me to take two more horses, so you can ride one."

He nods. Leo comes strolling up, sniffing Mitch. He makes his happy wolf face after a second. Mitch squats to scratch Leo's face, grinning up at me, "You know you need my skills anyway."

I snort, "It's sad, but you could be the difference between survival and not. We don't have a lot of snipers at the farmhouse."

He winks, "I hear you got a lot of ladies."

I fold my arms over my chest, "We do. You know how to deliver a baby?"

He smiles, standing up, "I do. I did it once. It was scary as shit, but I can I do it."

I slap his arm, "Then you'll be popular."

His face blushes a little. He's normally the strong, silent type; he's me but a guy. Star strolls over, looking strong and confident, "You hear the towns have started up law enforcement?"

I frown, "They always had guards."

She shakes her head, "Sheriffs. They started swearing in sheriffs and judges. With no farms and camps, and no city, the towns are becoming real towns. They're trying to get rid of the corruption."

I roll my eyes, "Kind of a day late and a dollar short." I read that in one of Granny's novels. I love that one.

She laughs, "It's better than nothing. We've been thinking since we have ten houses, we might do the same. You guys should too."

I look at Mitch, "You wanna be my sheriff?"

He nods once, "I'd do anything for you, Em."

The comment makes me uncomfortable, just a little. I pretend it's nothing and nod, "Okay."

Star points at Sully, I barely recognize him. He's a beast of a man somehow. In the month I've been gone, he has gained massive amounts of muscle, like Star, but more bulging. "He wants you guys to take four horses, one is a stud and not related to any of the females at the farm."

I nod, "Okay. Just tell Jake what you want. He's the horse guy."

She laughs, "Who knew he had a purpose, beyond making the view that much better."

I laugh.

She winks, "Studding horses suits him." She walks away and her shorts and tee shirt suddenly suit her. Her body is strong and fit now. She doesn't giggle and she doesn't hug people. She slaps them on the arm.

"She's so different now."

I glance at Mitch and nod, "So different."

He swallows, "I almost miss the giggly massage girl."

"You know that was an act right? That never was who she was. She was trying to blend in, keep information flowing from Marshall and her brother."

He gives me a smirk, "I know. I still liked that sweet smile and funny laugh."

I sigh, "Men are animals."

He laughs and walks with me to Jake. Sully's sees us, his dirty face brightens, "Emma!"

I wave but he comes over, giving me a bulging, muscled, and sweat-laden hug. My back cracks when he shakes me.

He puts me down, "How's Will, Anna, and Sarah?"

"Great. They're all great. Anna is getting a small belly. It's like a tiny little hump. And she's not sick anymore."

He smiles, "Cool. Me and Star wanna get some officials around here, so that when the little bambino comes we can come up there." He nods behind the barn, "We're making a cart into a sled. You all should do the same thing."

"Smart. I'll tell Will."

His eyes narrow a little, "How's he feeling?"

I shake my head, "He doesn't say much. You know what he's like."

He snorts, "Yeah, he's you, but he's got a dick."

I frown.

He laughs. I don't see what's funny about that statement. Sometimes I still get lost in conversations, but I've come a long way.

Mitch nudges me, "Emma doesn't like talking about dicks, she likes killing shit."

My face is getting red. I glance at Meg's grave where Leo is sitting alone and point, "I'm going to say hi to Meg." I walk past them and try to not hear their laughing.

It takes me a minute to pull the dead branches and leaves off the mound of rocks. Leo sits, looking regal. His eyes always get sad when he's with her.

I kneel beside him and run my hands down his back.

I don't look down into the rock pile though. I look up and smile, "Hey, Meg."

I know she's there. I know very few things, but I know that.

After a minute Jake is there beside me. The warmth of his body next to mine is nice.

"Hi, Meg."

Leo whines a little and lies down. Jake nods his head. I can tell he's saying something in his head. I reach over, taking his hand in mine. He doesn't look at me but he squeezes.

I hear boots behind us, "Wanna take a hot shower? I got the power up and running now. The inverter is finally fixed."

I glance back at Star, "Seriously?"

She grins.

Jake winks at me, "I'll race you to the showers."

I stick my tongue out, "Just go first. My legs are broken from that damned horse."

He helps me up, "No, you go first."

Star laughs, "Always the gentleman."

His eyes burn, "Not always."

Chapter Twelve

The next day the saddle instantly picks a fight with my butt. I wince and wait for the numb to take over again.

Mitch laughs, "Oh, that was a face. Sore arse, Emma?"

I growl and give him a hard look. He puts his hands up defensively but continues laughing.

Jake gives me a shitty grin too. I snarl and nod at Star, "I'll send word when the snow hits, and if anything remarkable happens."

She winks, "I'll send word if I find Daddy Dearest."

I have created a monster. She is more like me daily, like she's picking up the cold hateful pieces I am losing. I nod, "Don't go after him without me." I don't want him to kill her. We may not be close, but she's all I have left. She's my blood.

She slaps the butt of the horse, "Have a safe trip." My horse leaps into action. I almost cry out. I need to learn to ride horses better. Flopping around in the seat might be the death of me.

Sully waves us off at the gate. I can't make myself trust him. He does everything he can to earn our trust and help us, but to me he was one of them. I have to force myself to see Jack when I look at him. No matter what, I see the picture I made in my head of them eating people. It makes me gag a little.

Mitch and Jake pass me, making dust for me to follow. I see movement to the right as we pass the crater. I pull an arrow and make an attempt at the matted, red hair of the monster stumbling along the grass. I loose two arrows but they both miss. Leo looks at me and then sprints off to the side. He snaps her neck and catches up to me. I sigh, I need to learn to shoot from a horse. This is my new goal.

We pass the place where Fish and the gang captured us, and I try again on a deer running alongside the destroyed road. I'm going to run out of arrows at this rate. Leo doesn't even attempt the deer. I think he's starting to feel sorry for me so he's pretending to not see my sucky aim.

The guard on the platform in the tree is an amazing sight. He waves at us as we ride in. Jake has the extra horse tied to him so he goes directly to the right when we break the forest. The farmhouse and the small village look bigger than before. More people maybe.

Will comes out smiling. He looks red, not burnt, but winded. I'm going to smack him around. He grabs my horse's reigns but smiles at Mitch, "Hey, man. How's it going?"

Mitch hops off his horse like we just did a quick jaunt around the yard. He doesn't look like he might die any second. I can't get off the horse fast enough, but when I do my legs buckle. Leo is there when I fall. I lean on his huge back, "Thanks, buddy."

Mitch and Will are hugging. I can see relief on Mitch's face. "I heard you were gone, brother."

Will glances at me, "Yeah, I was for a little while."

Mitch smacks his arm, "Even the devil didn't want you, huh?"

Will chuckles, "Naw."

Mitch sees Anna, I see the sadness on his face. He nods that way, "Going to go see how the momma-to-be is doing."

Will turns to me, "Sore butt?"

I want to whine and soak it in hot water. I sigh, "It hurts."

He pulls me into his arms, rubbing my butt gently, "Come on. I'll give you a butt massage."

I shove him away, "No. I can tell you're all sweaty and red. You didn't relax."

He grabs my arm, knowing I hate that and plants a kiss on my lips. I can feel the challenging smile on his lips, "Come relax with me."

I shake my head, "That's not relaxing."

He laughs and wraps his arm around me, pulling the horse to the pen.

Anna gives me a sad look; she's talking to Mitch but I can see something is wrong.

"What's up with Anna?"

He sighs, "She's been having cramps all day. She thinks she's going to lose the baby."

The words trigger something in my mind, "Bed rest."

He frowns, "What?"

I nod, "Bed rest. My mom was scared she was losing me; the doctors put her on bed rest."

He frowns, "Really?"

"Yeah. You get the horse and I'll get the pregnant, crazy woman into bed."

He swats me on the butt. I growl but it just makes his eyes flash with humor.

Nearly limping, I make it over to her and point at the house, "Come with me."

I take her hand and pull her inside. She tries to pull back but I don’t relent. My butt is killing me, my legs are exhausted, and I'm moody and hungry. I get to the back rooms and pull her into the one that she sleeps in alone. I close the door and point at the bed, "Bed rest."

She whispers, "What?"

I nod, "Bed rest. My mom was sure she was losing me and the doctors put her on bed rest. You had the infection, you shouldn’t even be able to have babies. You need to stay on bed rest."

Her face drops, "Em, I'll go nuts in here."

I shake my head, "You have to choose, baby or sanity."

She kicks her boots off and climbs into the bed. She frowns, "I need books. That Da Vinci one was good, but I'm out."

I nod, "I'll get books. You sit."

She wrinkles her nose, "How long do I have to stay in here?"

I shrug, "I don't know. I guess until you feel normal again. Lay back so then the baby can't fall out."

She laughs and curls up on the bed. I can see she's exhausted.

I kick my boots off too and climb onto the bed with her. She grimaces, "You smell like horse."

I grin, "Yeah, well I had a shower yesterday at Star's, so I should smell like the lavender shampoo they're making there."

Her eyes bug open, "The hot water is back?"

I nod.

She moans in a wheezy whisper, "Oh, man. I need a hot shower. I made Nan heat me water on the fire and pour it on me, but it wasn't the same."

I close my eyes, "It was amazing."

She whispers against my face, "You ever miss the breeder farm?"

I smile, "Yup."

The door opens. I glance back to see Sarah. I laugh, "Speaking of missing the breeder farms."

Sarah kicks her shoes off and climbs on the bed with us. "Will said you were back." She curls in between me and Anna. "I don't miss the farms, I miss the cook."

I laugh and close my eyes again.

I don't dream, I sleep completely peacefully. When I wake, I'm next to Will. I open my eyes to see him staring at me. He must have moved me in the night. He runs a hand down my cheek. I smile and close my eyes again. He wraps an arm around me, pulling me into him.

"You smell good."

I moan, "Mmmm, I had a shower at Star's. She knew Bernie had kept a bunch of solar panel stuff in the metal bunker under the house. The H.E.M.P. didn't ruin it. She had to get something called an inverter fixed and then have it all hooked up. I didn't think she'd be able to do it, but she did."

"They have power?"

I nod.

He makes a whistle sound, "That's dangerous."

I open my eyes, "Why?"

He shakes his head, "Baby, we never want to have more than anyone else. We don't want to have the things they don't. If we have just enough to live, then no one is going to come and attack us and try to take it. People see power and then they want to rule."

"But she's going to get sheriffs and law enforcement. Maybe if they have some hangings or shootings, the bad people will stay away."

He shakes his head, "Not smart. Marshall was smart, how he did it. The camp and retreat were based entirely upon the group being a council and us only ever having what we needed. We were never the target of bandits or raids. We had a good population but not too much stuff."

I feel myself nodding off again, "It's sad we can't ever have anything ever again."

I sleep through the night, waking to Leo shifting on the bed. Will is wrapped around me totally and Leo is on my feet. I wrestle out from under them both and climb out of bed.

My legs are better and my butt doesn't hurt anymore. There is definitely a perk to being me.

I pull on my boots and Will's long-sleeve shirt. It smells like him, his stink that, for whatever reason, I like.

I stroll out into the kitchen. Nan smiles, "Hey, kid."

I nod, "Morning."

Her eyes dart to the right, "They caught someone on the property this morning."

I look at the door and think about what Will and I had talked about. I strap my holsters to my thighs and walk out of the house, "Just one person?"

She nods.

Mitch gives me a look from across the gravel yard. I see a young man with long, dark hair. His dirty face is thin and tired looking. When he sees me, his eyes get trapped, staring at the guns on my legs.

I sling my bow and quiver over my shoulder and crunch my way to where Mitch is.

"Found us a friend in the woods. The guards caught him."

I stare at the dark eyes of the young man and nod, "Execute him."

Mitch's jaw drops, "He could help around here."

I shake my head, "This isn't a work camp; we don't keep slaves." I walk to the guy, wiping my hand down the dirt on his face, "This dirt was rubbed on. I bet he followed us yesterday. He's a scout." I lift his lip, discovering perfect, white teeth. I give Mitch a look, "Take him behind the barn. I'll execute him."

Mitch scowls, "Em, you don't want to do this."

I grab the arm of the guy from Mitch, "I'll do it myself then."

The guy's mouth opens, "Fine, fine. She's right. I'm a scout. We fled from the city; we knew where the retreat was. It was on a map. Please, I'm a doctor."

My eyes narrow, "You're twenty—how could you be a doctor?"

His eyes search mine for compassion. I know he's going to come up empty. He flinches at my cold stare, "I was apprenticing under some of the doctors in the city. I was learning to be a breeder doctor."

His eyes are crystal clear, like mine and Star's, "You're a Gen baby."

His eyes narrow for a second but he doesn't say anything. His lips press together.

I reach up, grabbing his shirt, "ARE YOU?"

"YES!"

I jerk him back and release him, "Shit." I look at Mitch, "He's my brother, but he's from the city. Send scouts into the woods."

The guy's eyes get nervous when I say it. He makes a face and then smiles, "You're Emma."

I grab his thick arm and drag him to the barn and point at the bunker in the floor, giving Mitch a deadly look, "Open that."

Mitch gives me a look but he does it. I push my new brother down into the hole and slam the lip. His green-blue eyes are the last thing I see of his face. I click the latch on the bunker and run my hands over my face, "Shit."

Panic is filling me. My father might be in the woods, or at Bernie's. Of course he would know where the retreat was and where Bernie lived. I slap my forehead, "Stupid, stupid, stupid."

Mitch grabs my arm, "Em, chill out. It's one guy."

I shake my head, "No. The city burned; they have nowhere to go. They've never been out here in the wild. They know where we've set up camp and villages. They had a room filled with maps. They know where we live." I can hear the panic in my voice.

I point down at the lid covered in hay, "That is not a scout—it's a test. Test to see how fast we respond, how we act, and what kind of place we are, so they know what they need to take this from us."

Mitch puts his hands on my arms, "Calm down. Your crazy is showing. This is one guy, one doctor. You could beat him up, he doesn't stand a chance here. Stay calm."

I take a deep breath and nod, "Okay. But I want pairs into the woods, finding them. I know there are more."

He nods, "Okay. Me, you, and Leo will be one pair, okay? We'll do the perimeter."

I go to whistle for him but Will opens the kitchen door, giving me and Mitch a weird look. Leo leaves the kitchen, sauntering to me. He sniffs the door to the bunker and growls.

I step out of Mitch's arms and point at the bunker door, "A scout from the city."

Will closes his eyes, "Shit." He points to the field, "We need scouting parties out. I want pairs to do a five-mile hike. Me, Em, and Leo will take one route. Mitch…"

I cut him off, "Will, me and Mitch are going together. You need to rest; me and him can run this perimeter with Leo fast. You need to rest."

His eyes dart between me and Mitch. He nods and walks back into the house, slamming the door.

Mitch sighs, "He thinks shit is going on, doesn't he?"

I shake my head, "That's not so important right now. Let's do this and I'll talk to him afterwards."

Mitch laughs, "This is your first boyfriend isn't it? Go talk to him now."

I don't want to. I don't want to see the angry look on his face, or even worse, the pathetic one. I hate that look.

Mitch shoves me, "Get going, chicken shit."

I growl and walk into the house. Nan makes a muttering noise as I walk past her, ignoring it. He's in the bedroom, getting boots on. I close the door behind me and pressing my back into it.

He doesn't look at me. He walks to the door, like he might move me or walk right through me.

I flinch when his hand moves. It stops him, but I can see his face get red. "You think I would hit you?"

I shake my head, "No."

I don't wait for him to act nuts. It makes us both nuts and I'm tired of that song and dance. I wrap my arms around his neck and kiss his throat. He remains wooden.

I bite him softly, smiling against his skin, "Just say the thing you think."

He shakes his head.

I climb him like a huge tree, wrapping my legs around his waist. I close my eyes and whisper into his ear, "I don't know how to say it, Will. I don't have that thing that I need to tell you how I feel, but I know how I don't feel. I know the things I can't live without. Don't make me shoot you."

He scoffs. I can feel him softening. His hands creep along my legs, cupping my butt. He holds me to him, pressing his face into mine. "I don't have a purpose, Em. It's making me nuts."

I pull back, "You have a purpose. You make these people trust this place and me. You are the figurehead. You're the brains; you don't need to be the brawn anymore."

He laughs, "Nothing like taking the man out of me."

I laugh too, "You know what I mean."

He shakes his head, "Next time can you just shoot me? I think it might be less painful than listening to this speech."

I shake my head, "No." I kiss his cheek, "Now I'm gonna go do a perimeter check with Mitch, my friend, and then I'm going to torture my new brother."

He flinches, "What?"

I nod, "He's mine and Star's age and from the city. His eyes are clear like ours, and I swear I can see Michael in his face. I asked him if he was a Gen baby and he said yes."

Will places me down, "Great. This is just getting better and better."

I kiss his cheek, "It's like you said. They are going to try to take what's ours ‘cause we have it better than them."

He kisses my lips softly, "Em, they aren't taking anything."

I reach behind me and open the door, "Please, Will. Please rest. Don’t exert yourself. Your breathing has been sounding bad."

He nods, "Okay. Stay with Leo."

I wink at him like Jake always does, "Done."

I leave the house again, worrying about everything.

Mitch gives me a shitty grin, "Was that so hard?"

Chapter Thirteen

The bark feels rough against my hands but the cool wind feels amazing. I can see Leo doing laps in the woods and Mitch in the tree to the right of me. Nothing else is moving though. We've run a perimeter and now I'm camped in my tree. Leo makes his way back to the meeting tree and sits at the bottom. He clearly hasn't gotten a scent or seen anything; he looks peaceful like we're playing.

I look down at Leo, "Guess we're going with torture."

He pants and smiles. He doesn't care either way.

I feel myself harden as I get back down on the ground. The forest sings around us. I leave the woods and stalk across the field, loving the feel of his fur in my fingertips as we walk. Mitch leaves the forest when he sees me walking in the tilled field.

The first thing I see is the lid of the bunker open when I round the corner. My guns are out instantly. Leo crouches low as we crunch our way to the farmhouse. Jake and a few guys are chatting in the horse pen and a girl with really blonde hair is feeding the goats. Men are hammering metal and no one seems to notice the bunker lid. He's snuck into the house maybe.

I open the porch door. Nan isn't there. No one is. I slip down the hall, peeking in the doorways. No one makes any noises. I open Anna's door, but even Leo doesn't want to look in there. The thing in the doorway is disturbing. I raise my gun at him, wincing in horror.

Anna frowns and wheeze yells at me. I can't understand her, but the doctor waves his free hand at me, "Her cervix is still closed. The cramps and bleeding are probably just spotting. You were right about the bed rest though."

His other hand moves between her legs. I gag a little bit, shaking my head. Anna snarls at me.

The doctor guy nods at the door, "Close the door. She says if Will sees, she's going to be pissed."

I stumble back. Leo has abandoned me. I close the door, still holding my guns out.

"Emma, would you stop. Jeeze, you act like such a boy sometimes."

I look down the hallway at Nan and shake my head, "What was that?"

She laughs, "Well, I figured why lock the doctor up, we can just get him to check out Anna real quick before you kill him. So I got Jake to let him out." I snarl but she points a thick wooden spoon at me, "Now you better not give me that look, young lady. I'll slap you around. I am not taking that shit off of you."

I point, hearing the way my voice cracks, "Nan, he's a monster. He's like me but worse. He's on Michael's team. He's probably killing Anna."

She rolls her eyes, "Through the vagina? Yeah, that's an efficient way to kill."

I gag as she says it and storm out of the house.

Will is crossing the field. My lip lifts when I see him talking to Mitch. I walk the other way. I know what is going to happen if I stay or confront him. I'm in the mood to shoot someone.

Leo rejoins me when we reach the forest's edge. I wave at the guy on the platform, "Take a break."

He nods and climbs down. I climb up and Leo finds himself a nice spot to make one of his nests. I see Jake crossing the field to where I am. When the tree sways, I clench my jaw. He climbs onto the platform, grinning away.

"Will send you?"

He nods, "You know it. He's a chicken shit when it comes to you angry."

I mutter, "I need to shoot him again, I think." I give him a look, still listening to the sound of the forest, "You know that guy is a bad man."

He shakes his head, "No, he isn't. He's a scout who won't make it back. He's been training to become a breeder doctor; Anna is a breeder, whether we like it or not. She is having that baby, against my wishes. It's better to have someone here who knows what they're doing."

I scoff and look down at Leo. He is still curled in a ball.

Jake tosses a balled-up leaf at me, "You need to stop being so paranoid. Maybe everything is going to work out. Maybe this is a safe place for us to be."

My stare darkens, "I don’t believe that place exists. I'm trying to, but I can't and he is a reminder that we are in danger at all times."

"Emma, you are so bad at being around other people sometimes. You gotta mellow out."

I scowl. I don’t know what that means.

He laughs, "My dad used to say that all the time to my mom—mellow out. It means calm down and be chilled out."

I get up to climb down and leave him up there, but Leo isn’t curled in a ball. He's staring at something in the forest and I don’t hear the forest song.

He chuckles, "I mean really…" I reach over and clamp his mouth shut, pulling him down to the platform on his belly. I lie beside him, keeping my eyes peeled to the forest. A crunch off to the left sends my eyes in that direction. I see Leo turn that way too.

I see the slightest flash of something between two trees. It comes out after another tree. It's a horse. The rider is slumped over the head of the horse. I jump up and start climbing down. Leo is already running in the direction. I shout up at Jake, "Sound the alarm."

He looks panicked for a second but gets up, and I hear the gong of the log against the sheet of metal we dragged up into the platform.

I jump into the duff on the forest floor and sprint into the trees.

I see her matted hair, soaked in blood and start to feel sick, "STAR!"

She lifts her bloody face, weakly and smiles, "Em."

I grab the reigns of the horse and see the second one behind her. It's empty. The rider has fallen off. I jump onto the back of the horse with no rider and pull Star's horse.

We ride across the dusty grass into the driveway that has become our courtyard. People rush towards me. Will pulls Star down. I don't look at him or her. I enter the house. Nan sees my face and moves. She knows better. I kick the back room door open. Anna is laughing and talking in her whisper. I grab the doctor guy and drag him down the hall. He shouts and screams, and Anna makes her wheezy noises. I point at Nan, "Keep her in bed. No matter what."

Nan nods once.

I drag the shouting man out into the yard. I point at my bloody sister, "WHAT THE HELL IS THAT?"

He sees her face, swallowing hard. I see the recognition in his eyes. He knows her face and what happened. He looks at me, trying to hide it, "I don't know."

I punch hard. He knocks back. The gathering crowd shouts. I feel someone grab at my arm, but it's too late. My rage is there; they get shoved back hard and my gun is out. I fire a shot into his thigh, "WHAT IS THAT?"

He screams, "I DON'T KNOW! I KNOW THEY WERE GOING

FOR THE SOLAR PANELS! I DIDN'T KNOW WHEN! I WAS TOLD TO CHECK YOU GUYS OUT AND GO THERE!"

I fire at his other leg, barely grazing it, "YOU COULD HAVE WARNED US!"

He screams again, "PLEASE, I DIDN'T KNOW WHEN! I SWEAR! I HEARD YOU WERE THE ONE WHO SAVED US ALL IN THE CITY AND I VOLUNTEERED TO COME HERE AS A SCOUT! I WANTED TO FIND YOU!"

I lift the gun into his face. Leo growls in front of me, snarling savagely.

Tears stream down his cheeks, "Please. I didn't have any part in that."

I feel something wrap around me. I assume it's Will about to rip my arms off, but it's Anna. She wraps herself around me whispering, "He's not bad. I know him. I met him at the farms. He snuck me to a different area, to make sure they put a baby in my belly. His name is Nick. Doctor Nick. Remember me telling you about Doctor Nick. He was the nice one. This is him. I was trying to tell you, when you were dragging him away."

My hand starts to shake. I lower it, seeing the stricken face on him. I nod at Star, "Fix yourself and her."

He nods, "Thank you."

I almost hit him with the gun, but I don't. I turn, seeing the way everyone is looking at me.

Mitch is holding Will back. I holster my gun and look at Star, "Did they overrun everything?"

She nods, looking like she might pass out any second.

"Do you think they'll stay there?"

She nods, "Michael wanted the mansion; he knew what Bernie had there. He doesn't care about us."

My eyes narrow. She sees the look, "Soon as I'm better." I stalk off, back to the platform. I can't look at Will and Anna. I know they're disappointed in me. I am too, but it's not for the same reason. I wish I'd killed Michael, when I had the chance. I should have known that letting him live would mean that he would find a way to still live the good life, and it would still be on the backs of the weak. I climb the tree and slump onto the platform. Jake giggles. It makes me smile.

"Did you shoot that nice doctor?"

I sigh and look down at Leo snuggling into a ball again, "Shit."

Jake nods, "That's about it."

The sun sets and someone brings food. Jake climbs down and gets it. He passes me the fresh bread and stew when he gets back up. I moan, "The food is getting better, I swear it."

He nods, "It is. At least Nan stopped trying to make goat butter. That was nasty."

I laugh, "We need a cow or two."

I see a dark figure limping across the field and wince, "Shit."

Jake looks and laughs, "This is going to be fun."

I hear Leo growl and the doctor struggle to get in the tree with the injured legs. He winces and moans, but makes it to the platform, dragging his body across it.

Jake reaches over and pulls him to sit with us.

"Hey."

The doctor tries to catch his breath, "Hi."

He presses his back against the wood of the platform railing, "So, I want to go to the mansion and tell Michael that this camp is a bust. It's a little shit show of people barely surviving."

I laugh, "No."

"They'll come here to look for themselves, if I don't."

I shake my heads, "I don't trust you. Anna may be fooled by

Doctor Nick, but I am not."

He sighs, "You will be bringing the small army Michael has down on these people. I can stop it."

I lean into him, "You are going to tell him exactly how to get here and exactly how to overrun us."

He looks at Jake, "Is she always like this?"

Jake grins, "Worse usually. This is her keeping her temper in check."

His eyebrows raise. His dark-blonde hair and dark-blue eyes remind me of family.

"How did you know you were a Gen baby?" I ask, ignoring their conversation.

He smiles, "I knew always. My mom died; Michael raised me at the lab and explained how much better I was than everyone else. When the world ended, Michael took us to a place to stay safe, while the city was being finished. Things happened faster than he thought they would. He wasn't as involved in the end of the world as he liked to think he was."

"Why did he let the seed Gen babies overrun the city and terrorize people?"

He frowns, "I think he sees them as superior. He doesn't see the flaws in the system. He thinks the weaker humans should bow down to them."

"How are you so calm?"

He sighs, "I'm not. I'm just not trained for combat, the way you are."

I chuckle, "I'm not trained for combat. My dad died when I was ten. This is me surviving."

Jake points, "It's similar to combat training though. I guarantee, if there were marines left, she would be one of them."

The doctor puts his hand out, "I'm Nick."

Jake takes his hand, "Jake."

I roll my eyes, "He came here to help Michael terrorize us, and you're shaking hands?"

Nick gives me a look, "I don't know how else to make you believe. I came here to seek you out. I was at the breeder farm where you were for a few weeks. I left about four days before you took it down. I would have helped you, if I had known that was what you were going to do."

I listen to the silence of the forest and shake my head, "I don't want your help."

"I can birth that baby for Anna and I can stop Michael from coming here."

I narrow my gaze, "How? Go there and tell him everything is shit here and we're toothless mountain people? Then what, genius? You think he's going to miss the fact you're leaving again?"

He shrugs, "I'll go with the next scouting party and run away when we attack. They'll think I died. I'll be back before it's time to birth the baby."

Jake nods, "This is a good idea."

I shake my head, "No. He stays and keeps Anna safe. That's the plan, or he dies. He doesn't leave the yard."

Nick smiles, "You really are a hard ass. You remind me of Michael."

I growl. Jake slides along the boards between us, "Whoa, let's not start name calling."

Nick's eyes burn, "I didn't mean it in a bad way. I meant it as a compliment. He had the potential to be someone amazing once. He let his God complex get to him. I don't think you have that flaw."

I grin at him, "I have others."

He laughs bitterly, "I am betting I haven't even seen half of them."

I stand up, "We haven't even scratched the surface." I toss Jake the rifle, "Don't shoot yourself." I climb down, trying to hide the fact I am a seething mess.

I want to go to my meeting tree but I don't. I decide to face the music. I walk up to the door of the house as someone clears their throat.

I glance behind my shoulder at Mitch standing in a shadow. His right eye is swollen shut. He points from the dark doorway of the barn, "You gonna kiss this better?"

I snort and press my back against the door, "Is Star okay?"

He nods, "She's fine. She's like you, heals quick."

"Aren't we the lucky ones?"

He shakes his head, "I don't think so. That irrational temper of yours isn't worth the fast healing."

I swallow, "Is Will okay?"

He laughs, "No. That's where I got this little gift. He's pissed. He sent Jake out to the tree; he knew he'd toss you over the edge."

I shrug, "I might win that fight."

He scoffs, "Not likely." He waves me off, "You better go face the music again." He slips back into the shadows, no doubt going to the loft to do his turn at the watch.

My stomach aches and burns, but I open the door, ignoring the look I get from the cook pit ladies. I give a simple nod and walk down the hall.

"We don't blame you."

I look back at them. The Jake dog gives me a happy look.

"We don't blame you. God knows what has become of our friends at the mansion. God knows what that monster is capable of."

I nod again, "Thanks."

I turn and walk down the hallway. I go face the really mean one first. She glares at me as I open the door. Leo jumps on her bed, trying to soften her for me.

She rubs his fur, glaring at me. I put my hands in the air, "I told him he can stay."

"After you shot him twice—how generous."

I sigh, "Anna, he's one of them. He's one of them, whether we see it or not."

She points at me, "You're one of them too!"

I close my eyes and pinch the bridge of my nose, "I'm worse. Night." I step out and close the door, leaving Leo in there to try to make her feel better.

I put my hand on the knob but the door flies open. Star stares at me from the doorway. I don't know what to say or think, so I go for the obvious, "You alright?"

She looks back at Will who is sitting on the bed with no shirt on in a pair of shorts.

His eyes are wide, guilty. It makes me sick, but I have to assume it's nothing. The fire burning inside of me is trying to explode, but I fold my arms over my chest, holding myself together.

She nods, "I will be. I'm healing quickly. You okay?"

I nod, "How bad is the village?"

Her eyes water, "Sully, uhm..." She starts to cry, "Sully is gone. He fought a lot of them and most of our people got away—they ran. They knew the trail through the bomb woods so when they got chased Michael's men got blown up. A lot of them are dead." A sickening grin crosses her lips, "It's probably only twenty men."

I laugh, "We can take twenty men."

She wipes her tears and shakes her head, "We gotta kill him. He's already planning shit. He's been taking the infected and releasing them on towns. Hordes of infected."

That was why he was caging them. I shake my head, "That

doesn’t even make sense. He's just making more of them."

She shrugs, "I don’t think he cares. I think he just wants the borderlands cleansed of people like them."

Will looks at us, "Night, Star."

She nods and gives me a sorry look, "Night."

She walks past me down the hall. I enter the room and close the door. Will gives me a hard look, "You want them to stay here, and then you scare the shit out of them when a single guys shows up. You know how many people wanted to leave today, terrified of when the crazy girl was going to snap and kill everyone?"

I swallow my defense and let him get pissed off. He's sweating again.

"You can't go around shooting people and acting nuts. You have to learn to use your words and not your hands." He coughs and I see something red fly from his lips. I look down at the blankets, "How long has that been going on?"

He shakes his head, "It's nothing. Just the old wound acting up."

I walk to him and press my hand against his face. He's hot like Jake was that one time. I close my eyes.

"Emma, are you listening to me? You can't keep acting like this. You have to try to not act like a psycho."

I block him out, trying to formulate a plan. I need a plan. He can yell at me later, I need something. I sit on the bed, covering my face with my hands and rock slightly.

"What are you doing? Have you lost your mind? Do you need some time in the bunker hole too?"

I block him out and get up from the bed.

"EMMA!"

I turn back to him, "You wait here. I'll be right back."

He tries to yell at me again, but he starts coughing. I leave him there. "Nan, he's sick. Lungs are infected, I think. Make him soup and get a ton of fluid into him. I'm sending the doctor there now."

She looks at me, startled, "You sure?"

I nod, "He's burning up and cantankerous, so be careful. I don't know if it's contagious. The house should empty. We need Anna out of here, in case though."

I leave the house. Star is in the barn door, talking to Mitch up in the loft. They stop talking to look at me. I walk across the dusty grass to the platform. I shout up into the dark, "Nick, can I ask you a favor?"

"You got some balls, Em."

I sigh, "Shut up, Jake. Nick, I need your help." I remember his legs and sigh, "Jake, help him down."

I hear Jake chuckle, "She's always this pleasant; it's not you. Trust me."

Chapter Fourteen

Star passes me a piece of dried meat. I take it without taking my eyes off of the village. There are far more than twenty men, but they are mostly not men. They're teenagers; I would imagine Michael's little army of doom is made up of Gen babies. Irrational little bastards like me and Star.

"Nick said Will has three or four days before we know if he's going to make it without medicine."

Star nods, "I bet Michael has some."

I look over at the gate, where Sully's head is mounted on a stake, and wonder how angry she is. I didn't even trust him and I'm pissed. Staking someone's head on a gate is sick and twisted.

"We can go in tonight, pretend to be one of them."

I point at the grounds, "How many women do you see?"

She glances around the whole village and scowls, "Misogynistic piece of shit."

I nod and chew the meat. Leo whines from the ground. I glance behind us to see a scout. I pull an arrow and take a breath as I sight it in. I release it, dropping him instantly. Star is out of the tree instantly. She takes his weapons and drags his body under a log before she climbs back up into the tree, without really making it sway.

I grin at her. She winks, swinging the gun over her shoulder. She pulls out a couple grenades with a grin like she found a candy bar.

I take one and leave her the other.

I chew the meat and tap my fingers against the tree, "We sneak in on the west side where the bombs are in the woods; they'll be more scared to go over there. That side door we went in last time, we go in there, and silently kill our way to him."

She nods, "Okay. Soon as it's really dark."

"I'll go tell Jake and Mitch."

She smirks, "Make sure Jake stays far away from here."

"Yup." I climb down the tree and make my way through the forest with Leo. Jake is sitting on the far side of the woods with the four horses.

He smiles when he sees me. He doesn't look behind me to make sure I wasn't followed, or even look around himself. He has a gun to keep him safe from the infected, more though, he has Mitch.

"We're going in when it gets quiet and everyone goes to bed."

Mitch nods, "I'll come with you."

I shake my head, "No. You need to keep him safe."

Jake rolls his eyes, "I'm not tits on a bull, Em. I can help. That's a lot of dudes, let us help."

I give Mitch a look. He nods. I turn and walk back into the woods.

We wait until the dark of night has settled in, and the camp has completely died down, and then make our way into the woods. I have double blades, handguns, my bow and quiver, and a rifle. She has the same, minus the bow. It's almost the last of the weapons from our camp.

I follow her perfectly through the bomb path. I'm sure Bernie made her run it many times.

We stop at the weapons hold to see if even a few things have been left there. She finds a couple protein bars, some ammo, and a bigger knife.

I eat the protein bar too fast and burp it the whole way along the woods. I hear the guard in the trees shifting as we get closer, and I pull an arrow silently. The only sound that we hear is the release of the arrow as it whips through the wind, and then slices into his head. It took a second for my eyes to adjust, but as he falls from the tree without making much noise, I know I hit the right spot.

Star takes his weapon, staying low. No one comes, even with the little bit of rustling that occurred.

We sneak along the new log house, hearing the people sleeping inside. The door at the side of the house opens without a sound. Star sneaks in and moves to the side, so Leo can get ahead of us. He waits in the hallway as I make my way into the first room on the right. I can hear the sleeping people.

We made an arrangement when we arrived, no one would be spared, regardless of what we found in those rooms.

I don't think as I slide my blade against the first throat I find.

It's just like the breeder farms; these are the ones who are against us. It's us and them. It always was.

Star takes the left and I take the right. We meet at the end of the hall, both looking haunted and hollow at the same time.

We slip into the kitchen and the shelter but no one is sleeping down there.

Leo takes the stairs. I hear a noise and a crunch, and see his yellow eyes glistening in the dark. We creep upstairs into the first room, the one I always slept in. I know the door has a creak. I open it quickly, the creak is there, but only for a second. Star hurries into the room, making the slicing sound, and the wet noise fills the darkness. Leo makes his crunching sound once. He's not eating them, just tearing the throat out in one fast bite. It isn't his first time killing without sound.

Sweat coats my face. I wipe it with my shirt and continue to the next room. Star opens it slowly. I creep past her, almost tripping on the person on the ground, sleeping on the floor. I take a knee and feel for their breath. I reach my hand for their throat, wishing everything were different. I'm loosing my edge. Star is done both people on the bed and someone on the floor, and I still haven't killed the person breathing on my hand. Leo senses my hesitation and finishes the job for me.

The next two rooms are the same. I don't have the fury and

vengeance Star has. The man I love is dying, but his head is not mounted on the gate of this village. She kills without thought or feeling. She has become numb to the pain of others. I almost envy her that; I miss that feeling a little. I miss turning my back on them and being responsible for me and Leo.

I don't know how to get that back.

We tiptoe to the back room that used to be Bernie's. It is the place that mine and Star's niece or nephew was created. It is the place where my best friend lost her virginity the right way, to the man she loved.

I can only assume Michael is in there.

Star looks at me in the dark; I see her eyes glisten with hatred and pain.

She nods once and creeps into the room. I follow her in, letting Leo take the lead though. We sneak to either side of the bed, moving perfectly, even without speaking. Who knew we would be the perfect assassination team. I suspect Michael did. I suspect he made us to be what we are.

The moon shines in the window slightly, making it easy to see the two women in his bed. He is in the middle of them, sleeping like a baby.

I grimace and glance at Star. She has the same face as me. Star slices the throat of the first girl. I can't. I know that. She doesn't look older than we are.

Star comes to my side and ends the girl for me, giving me a dirty look.

I shake my head and walk to the far side of the wall. I slide down it, Leo comes and sits next to me.

Star sits in the chair against the wall next to me, and we wait for him to wake and realize he's being bathed in the blood of the two girls he, no doubt, just took advantage of. I know what women will do for protection. It makes me sick.

The night is silent. No one in the house stirs or realizes that the whole main house has been murdered.

Michael moans and stirs, sliding his arm across the wetness of the body on the right, He lifts his hand and his face, sitting up abruptly. Star switches on the light next to her.

"Sleep well?"

His jaw drops and then his lips curl into a tight smile. He shakes his head, "The first ones were the best ones. There is no doubt. We used the best DNA from the top scientists and athletes in the world, making a cocktail of excellence. Of course, when they found out why we were doing it, they all backed out. Such a waste of talent that was."

Star lifts a gun from her lap, "We don't need your 'why I'm so evil and genius' speech. We just wanted you to know it was us who murdered you."

He laughs, as if either buying time or not believing us capable. "All the greatest have died for their beliefs or because they made their creations too amazing. You girls are prime examples of that. Think of the world you can create from the ashes of this one."

Star steadies her hand, "We aren't you. We don't want to make anything."

He puts his hands up, "I can give you anything and everything. It'll only be a matter of months before we are rebuilding the next city." His eyes sparkle, "Did you meet your brother, Nicholas? He is my prodigy, in every way. I sent him to see how you were doing."

My insides tighten.

His smile widens, "You have met him. You weren't foolish enough to let him in, were you?" He shakes his head, "Tsk, tsk, tsk, Emma. I expected more from you. Star here had a privileged life, what with Bernie being my right-hand man and all."

Leo bares his teeth. I almost bare mine.

Star fires the gun, "Not too privileged. I still learned how to shoot a gun, Dad." Michael jerks back from the bullet. I stand up, terrified and angry in a whole new way. If Anna, Jake, or Sarah are hurt because of Nick, I will never find my way back to the good place in my mind.

Michael winces as he coughs and then laughs. The bullet must have missed the important stuff. He looks like he might be able to get up off the bed. I lift my bow and pull an arrow.

He smiles at me, "I made you to be more, Emma. Stop devaluing what I created. Be the leader you naturally are. I've had everyone call you the phoenix, in preparation for you to be the one to take my place."

"So it was you that started the stupid nickname? You arrogant bastard. Granny and Gramps and Lenny were always right about you. Not worth the price of spit was how Granny always said it."

His eyes narrow.

I shake my head, sliding the arrow into the bow, "You didn't make me, Michael. God did. You donated sperm and tried to create something, but my mother and Lenny, Granny, and Leo made me. I am what I am because of them. You had no hand in that. I don't have to be the monster you tried to make. Granny and my real dad taught me about right and wrong." I smile peacefully, "And you aren't God, asshole. You're dead."

He opens his mouth, but I release the first arrow into his shoulder, " staring at the pupil of his eye as the second arrow pierces it.

Star switches off the light and opens the bedroom window. She waves at me, "This way." She opens a panel on the wall and puts her grenade inside, "Give me yours."

I pull it out and pass it to her.

We can hear the footsteps on the stairs of people coming to save Michael. No one is bringing his ass back from this. Bastard. I follow Leo out the window, onto the ledge. Star leaps out the window, "Run!" We sprint in the dark to the back of the house. She drops down onto the roof of the pantry and then onto the ground. Leo and me follow her into the woods. We run as fast as we can. I hear a gun cock behind us. My back tenses, waiting for the bullet to hit, but instead, I hear a whistle and something falling in the woods. I look back, but I can't see what it was.

We get a little further along to see Jake holding a bow and quiver, standing on a stump. We both stop, even Leo looks surprised.

He grins, "Now that was an impressive shot. Dummy used a scope, so easy to see him when the moonlight reflected off of it."

I smile, shocked and impressed. Mitch steps up onto the stump and shakes his head, "Gimme the bow back, you little shit."

Jake laughs quietly, "I totally had you fooled. Even Leo bought that one. You all owe me a coke for falling for that."

We saddle up and look at the house. Star raises the rifle, sighting it in and takes a breath. On the exhale she fires. The whole mansion explodes.

We stand there stunned as the camp erupts into flames and alarm. Secondary explosions start discharging. The entire property becomes a war zone of fire and screams.

Star kicks her horse into a fast run.

Mitch looks stunned, "What the hell was that?"

She looks back, "Bernie was paranoid. He never wanted his work to fall into the hands of the wrong people."

It makes a smile break across my face, but then I remember what he said about Nick. I boot my horse in the flanks shouting back at them, "Nick's a mole—we can't go get the medicine for Will. We have to go back first."

Jake looks at me from his saddle and shouts, "WHAT?"

I point, "NICK IS A MOLE! WE GOTTA GO BACK FIRST!"

He winces and I see his lips form the word shit. It’s our favorite I think.

Chapter Fifteen

We reach the guard platforms, but I don't see anything. No one is in the tree.

I feel sick as I round the corner and no one is in the yard. Of the nearly fifty people we left there, no one is around.

I leap from the horse, blasting into the house.

"ANNA, WILL!" No one answers.

Jake, Star and Mitch are doing the same. We meet back in the yard but there is no one.

The yard and house are empty. I turn and run down to the bedroom, smacking myself in the forehead; Anna can't yell. I push her door out of the way and stop when I see the bloody mess on the bed of the otherwise empty room. I grip the wooden frame of the door, stunned and disturbed as a thousand possibilities run through my mind.

Jake drops to his knees when he reaches the room. His face is buried in my side.

"EMMA!" Star sounds panicked.

I turn, running hard for the doorway, to where Star is staring across the field, pointing.

I see the group of them, all of them walking across the field. They look solemn and sad. Nick is in the front with Will and Anna.

I break into a run, but I don't stand a chance against Jake. They see us as we run, but they don't look excited about seeing us. I see mouths open to speak but we ignore them. Jake takes Nick to the ground, screaming and swinging.

Anna wheezes and screams as Will tries to pull him off of Nick. He has lost his mind. Will and some of the others wrestle him off of Nick, whose face is bleeding and swelling.

Anna grabs me, "I lost the baby. He didn’t hurt me." She knows what we saw in her room.

She points at the back lot and speaks in the high moan of the infected, "We made a graveyard."

My lip creeps out as tears start to fill my eyes. Star starts to cry. It's the last piece of Bernie, gone forever.

I pull her in and let her sob into me. Leo jumps up and wraps his paws around her. I don’t think he understands, but he always surprises me with his ability to sense things.

Sarah joins us, bawling too. Jake looks at me. I shake my head. He grabs Anna, holding her to him. Star finds her way into the embrace; she and Anna share their loss.

Will pulls me into him, "You okay?"

I shake my head, "I didn’t get the medicine yet."

He glances at Nick and offers him a hand, "Nick saved Anna."

I look into Nick's eyes apologetically, "He said you came to trick us."

He wipes blood off on his sleeve and pinches his nose, "Of course he did. He's a maniacal narcissistic asshole." He points back at the house, "Did you end him?"

I glance at Star's shaking body as she, Anna, and Jake hug and cry. I nod, "We did."

He offers me a bloody hand, "Let's start over then. Hi. I'm your half-brother, Nick."

I shake his hand, "I'm sorry I shot you."

He nods, "Yeah, it's been a rough week."

The people of our little village give us a sideways look and whisper amongst themselves.

Nick turns around and smiles, "The man who made the mess of our world has died. Emma and Star murdered him. We owe them a debt of gratitude."

The people look at Star, then me, and then each other. They don't look ready to thank me for ending the tyranny; I don't give a shit either way. I just want the whole world to stop fighting to be on top.

I turn away from them all and stagger to my friend. I wrap my arms around her and wish there was a way to change the losses she has suffered. It seems like the best of us have it the hardest. Anna is the best person in the world to me. She is the one who saved me as much as I saved her.

We slowly make our way to the houses and filter off into our different directions. Will wraps his arms around me and whispers, "Did you kill him?"

I nod, "I did."

His burning body next to mine scares me. I look at Nick, "Once, Michael told me that my blood could cure things."

His eyes sparkle for a second, "We need a needle to inject it."

I nod, "I know a place to get one." I give Mitch a smile, "Wanna go for a horse ride?"

He shakes his head, "No, my ass is killing me."

I scoff, "Well, we could walk."

He rolls his eyes, "I do not like you very much right now. I just need to put that out there."

"I don't care, you coming or not?"

He sighs, " Yeah."

I look up at Will, "Hang on for two days, okay?"

He shakes his head, "I'm fine, I swear. Me and Nick have been working on the lung thing. He doesn't even think it's contagious."

I give Nick a slight glance. His face tells me a different story.

I hug Anna once more, "I'm so sorry."

She shakes her head, "I should have known. The infection wrecked everything."

I kiss her cheek, "No, the important stuff is still there." I whisper into her ear, "If I don't come back, you make Nick keep him alive, okay?"

She nods.

I glance at Star, "I'm heading for needles."

She winks, "I know the best place." Jake gives us a look, "I'm coming too."

I glance at Will, who is talking to one of the cook pit ladies, "I need you to stay here and make him listen."

Jake shakes his head, "Anna can do that. Besides, I'll go nuts wondering what trouble you all are in without me."

Star rubs her butt, "How long before we leave?"

I shrug, "An hour."

She winces, "That's going to be horrid."

Mitch runs his hand over his butt too, "Mine doesn't hurt so bad. If you need a massage Star, I'm sure I could help you out."

Star cocks an eyebrow at him, "That's okay."

I walk to Will and take his hand in mine, "Come on."

He shakes his head, "I have a couple things to do in the barn. If the other smithy is gone, we need to fix this one up."

I smile, "Just come with me."

He gets a gleam on his fevered face. I pull him to Anna's room, "We need to clean this up. We can't make her do it."

He stops at the door and sighs, "Is it wrong I'm glad that she's not going to have a baby?"

I shake my head and start to gather the sheets. We clean everything and flip the mattress after we scrub it with the homemade soap.

The smell of blood and sadness washes away and leaves a lye smell. Will drags all the bedding to the group doing the laundry in the river's edge. I don't know how we'll do it in the winter, not with this many people. The well is amazing on this farm, but the population has grown a lot.

Mitch comes down the hall, "You ready? It's going to get dark soon."

I nod, "Yeah."

Anna comes down the hall, looking sleepy. Nick is beside her with a swollen face. His look tells me he wants to talk to me alone. I hug Anna and lead her into my room, "Sleep in here for a bit. You need to sleep to get better again."

She sighs, "I know. I'm just tired of being tired."

I hug her, "You'll feel better soon."

She squeezes me back, "I just wanted something of him."

I kiss her cheek and whisper, "You have his heart, Anna."

She starts to cry again, nodding, "I know." I give Nick a look. He stays in the hall as I take her into the room and tuck her into my bed. I kiss her forehead. Leo growls in the hallway and saunters in, jumping on the bed. He curls into a ball.

I rub his huge ears, "You stay with her, okay?"

He yawns and nestles into her better.

She closes her eyes, making tears stream down her cheeks. I leave, closing the door and leaning against it. Nick looks down, "I'm sorry, Em. I tried so hard, but there was no way."

I shook my head, "You said the cervix was closed."

He nods and closes his puffy eyes, "I'm scared it was me, putting my hand up there and touching it, might have made it worse.

Sometimes examining a woman who is about to lose a baby seals the deal."

I put a hand out on his arm, "Just keep her and Will alive. I don't give a shit about babies."

He snorts and looks at me. I swear his blue eyes have a hint of green in them and look similar to mine. He nods at me, "You really are cold sometimes. I see that hate fill you, like the breeder babies."

My gaze narrows, "Why don't you have that?"

He shakes his head, "I don't know. Some do and some don't."

I look down the hall, "I don't think Star has it naturally. I've seen it develop in her. She used to be different."

He nods, "It might be something that triggers in us, when we need it."

"Well then, I hope you never get it."

He laughs bitterly, "Me too." His look darkens, "How did you do it?"

"Arrow to the eye and then blew the house up."

He laughs, "Wow, so the whole place is gone?"

I nod, "It is. The breeder babies that were with him are gone too, mostly."

His stare meets mine again, "I will keep them safe and earn your trust. I swear it. I just want to be part of something good for a change."

"We'll see. But make no mistake..."

He cuts me off, "I know. You'll kill me and gut me like a fish, and burn me, and drag me behind a horse in the field. I've seen it, Emma—you're badass."

I laugh and slap his arm, "I've never had a real brother before. This might be fun, as long as you don't make me kill you." I walk past him to the yard and pray that he is the good person I'm betting he isn't.

Chapter Sixteen

I look back at them and wink. I like the winking thing. It makes me feel like I know something I definitely don't.

I walk from the woods, past the broken branches I did last time, and cross the broken highway where the bloodstains are still splattered on the cracked road.

I don't like being without my weapons, but I don't imagine the rules of the towns have changed much. What has changed is the blue-eyed guy next to me this time.

Jake looks nervous and smiles, "So we just walk in? They won't shoot us?"

I look up at him and smirk, "That's how it works usually. They want the trade so they don't normally kill the customers."

He doesn't look like it eases him at all.

We cross the road and I hear it; it still makes my stomach turn to stone.

The screams of the men who rip and tear fill the air. I see them running for us, hoping to rob us of whatever we have and rape me, of course.

Jake turns to run but I grab his hand. As the first ones get close, I see the bullets hit.

They drop mid-run.

I put my hands into the air so the guards see that it isn't me. Jake copies me, looking anxious and ready to run. The last couple thieves stop when they see the ten dead men on the pavement.

I glance at Jake, "This is easier with Mitch."

He swallows, "Was it like this last time?"

I nod. My eyes sparkle, "It was worse."

I can see him understand what I did for him as he shakes his head but has nothing to say.

We cross into the gates. The guard flashes me a grin, "Smart girl."

I give him a grin, "That wasn't me. Maybe it was God."

He snorts, "Welcome to the trading post."

Merchants don't rush at me like last time. They watch me from the lean-tos and shanties. I walk to the one where the old lady was. She sees me and scowls. I smile, "Surprised to see me alive?"

She mutters, "And yet, you came back." She sees Jake behind me and instantly her face splits into a grin, "But this time you brought me something I would be willing to trade for."

I look back at Jake. He gives me a clueless look. I smirk, "Yeah, he's not for sale."

She shrugs, "Too bad. We would pay by the pound for something that beautiful and that size."

Jake frowns, "What?"

I laugh, "I need needles and if you have any of the antibiotics left, I need that too."

A slow smile creeps along her old face, "Well, someone went and destroyed all the farms and labs so the antibiotics are all gone."

My hand lashes out fast, grabbing her throat and lifting her to her toes, "I have things to trade."

She gags and sputters but breaks out into a laugh. I toss her back into the stacks of trash bags. "I know where your son is."

Her eyes widen, "LIAR!"

I shake my head, "I know where he is."

She scrambles up, "How—how do you know where he is?"

I remain stoic.

"I can get you needles but the antibiotics are gone. Everything is gone. The power hasn't been on here in a while, but I can get you the needles. Where is he?"

She grabs for me, but I shove her back, "He's dead. I killed them all. You want to know who ended the power and the farms? It was me. I murdered every doctor I saw."

She screams and leaps for me, but I drop her skinny body to the ground and hold her there, "I did it especially for you. You and the other people of this shit hole, who traded the girls to the farms and camps." I get off of her. She is trembling and twitching, but still manages to pull a knife from under her dress. She leaps at me but Jake grabs her arm and bends it to stab the knife into her chest. He freezes and steps back.

She gags and opens her mouth to scream but she can't; he must have stabbed into her lung. Blood fills her mouth and she drops to the ground.

He's about to freak out. I point his face at mine, "Thank you."

He stops, realizing he saved me. His eyes dart back to the dying woman. I shake my head, "Trust me, she earned this fate."

He swallows and nods, "Okay." He doesn't believe me, but he never sat in the woods, terrified and listening to the screaming girls begging for death over the farms and being loaded into the trucks. I did.

Her body stops making sounds. I step over her and start to rifle through her cabinets. I open a drawer and a moth flies out. I wave it away and see the needles with plastic wrap on them still.

I sigh, "Found them."

Jake points at the now-dead woman, "What about her? They're going to know we killed her. The guards will kill us."

I smirk at him, "I know another way out. Come on." I drag her body to the back of the so-called store and bury her in the bags of garbage.

I stuff the needles in my sack and walk out into the street. The noise of the town is louder than before. People are bustling about and the merchants are shouting about their goods. I walk to the inn, keeping my head down.

The lady with the nice teeth smiles up from behind the bar, but doesn't really look at me, "No purchase, no room."

"I came to tell you that my virtue is no longer at risk."

Her eyes lift and her face breaks into a huge grin, "You're still alive."

I smile back, "Not for long. I just killed that old lady who betrayed me last time."

She winces, "Oh, that was a bad move. You came here right afterwards?" I nod. She shakes her head, "Thanks, kid." She gives Jake a sly smile, "Now tell me that was the person you were buying antibiotics for."

I nod, "It was."

Her eyes roam his whole body slowly, "That was worth it then."

I glance back at Jake and smile. His face is bright red but his eyes are still processing the fact he murdered a woman. I know some of the spark that makes him shiny and fun is going to die out. For him, killing her was like rubbing the magic dust off of a butterfly; he won't ever fly as high as before.

"We need the tunnel, just in case."

She winks, "What have you got for me?"

I smile, "Freedom."

Her gaze narrows, "What?"

I nod, "I killed Michael and burned the city to the ground and we have created a small village, where people are free and equal. I am offering you a place to live there."

Her eyes shine. She looks like she might turn me down, but she ducks behind the counter and comes up with a sack. She hurries around the counter, "I knew saving you would be a good idea."

She points to the stairs, "Hurry up."

I run up the stairs and enter the bedroom I slept in last time. She follows and closes the door. Jake looks lost, but as she opens the closet, his jaw drops.

I nudge him, "Her husband was a government man."

He nods, "Wow."

She puts a hand out, "I'm Stella, by the way."

I laugh, "Emma, and this is Jake."

She licks her red lips, "Well Jake, you are a tall drink of water, aren't you?"

His cheeks are burning, "Yeah, I get that a lot."

She nods, "I bet you do." I lead the way down the stairs into the tunnel and she closes everything up. I run, dragging my hand along the wall until I see the circle of light again. I climb the small ladder and push the hatch slowly. Nothing moves as I open it fully, and climb out into the fading light of the sun.

Jake comes out next and reaches down into the hole to help Stella. She smiles and looks different in the real light of the outside world.

I run towards where I know Mitch is sitting.

Star steps out from behind the tree where I stashed my weapons last time, "What is this?"

I nod, "Stella, she's one we want on our side." I point, "Stella, this is Star, my sister." Mitch jumps out of the tree, making Stella smile again. She puts a hand out to him, "Stella."

Mitch grins, "Mitch."

She gives me a smirk, "You run with the most handsome men, Emma."

I laugh and Mitch's cheeks turn scarlet. I point at the trail, "We've got a long ride home."

She rides with me, gasping as we enter the dusty field. "This is your village?"

I nod. She beams, "It's perfect."

I smile back at her, "It is."

Nick meets us in the driveway. His eyes tell me to get off my horse fast. I jump down, pulling the sack of needles from the saddlebag.

"Is he okay?"

He shakes his head, "No. We need to hurry. Did you find antibiotics?"

I shake my head, "Just needles. The power going out and the farms being shut down, ended the antibiotics."

His eyes narrow. He grabs the sack and runs inside the house. I follow him, ignoring everything else in the world.

Will is laying on the bed with Leo. His skin is flushed and sweaty, like Jake's was. I know Jake is behind me. I can feel the heat of his massive body there. I lean back into him as Nick gets the syringe out and sticks it into his own arm. He pulls the blood back into the needle until it fills. He pulls it out and presses a piece of cloth against it. He pulls down the sheet on Will's body and pushes the needle into the scar tissue on Will's chest and injects the blood.

"Give me your arm."

I put it out, he does the same to me and injects it too. Nick does my other arm and then his. When he finishes putting the fourth needle of our blood into Will, he sits and stares.

"Will it work?" I ask.

He shakes his head, "I don't know. I know in theory it should, but I don't know. Michael was a nut. He had it work on minor infections, like slivers. Our blood type is the kind we can give it to everyone." He looks down and back at me, "Unless he's a negative, then he's screwed. We're O positive."

Jake shakes his head, "Me and Will and Anna are all A positive. Dad told us that before he died. Same as our mom."

Nick nods, "Then this is the best chance he has." He doesn't sound convinced. He sounds scared and defeated. I back up to the wall and slide down it. Jake sits next to me. We sit there, staring at Will and waiting for it to work.

Eventually, they all leave and I sit alone. Even Leo doesn't want to watch it happen.

I climb up onto the bed and curl around him.

The heat from his body is intense and not lessening. I drip water into his mouth. He coughs and opens one eye. His lips crack when he tries to smile.

I don't smile back. I can't. I can see it. The blood isn't working. Michael was a crazy bastard, believing him was foolish.

"Em, stop looking so hateful. You want that to be the last thing I see?"

I lean into his chest, "Don't leave me. Please. I need you." I close my eyes and sob silently. I don't want my tears to be the last thing he sees either. I don't want there to be a last anything.

His hand weakly strokes my head. It isn't the same hand, or the same man, or the same love. It's all more. I know how far I can go into despair and darkness, and his death is one of the things that might push me there. I don't want to go back to being the person I was. I like the me that belongs with these people.

As if reading my mind he whispers, "Stop it. I made it back to you once, Em. I'll always be here. Not even death can keep me away."

I cry harder. I want to beg him not to leave me, but I can't speak. Nothing is working but my tears.

I hug him to me and pray to God that he leaves him here for me to love.

He grips my hand to him, "Look at me."

I lift my tear-stained face and shake my head.

He attempts a weak smile, but it gets lost in the pain and the fear I can see in his eyes. "Promise me, no matter what, you will stay with them and make an effort to not be crazy."

I snort and wipe my face. After a minute, I nod, "I won't ever leave them."

I see tears forming in his eyes as he struggles for the raspy words, "Keep Anna safe, and Jake."

"I swear I will."

He nods, "I know you will. My family is your family." He closes his eyes but mutters, "I love you, Emma."

My heartbreaks because I can hear the goodbye in his voice. I close my eyes too and rest my head on his chest. I don't know how long I lie there, before I realize his chest doesn't rise and fall anymore. The coarse sound of his breathing is gone.

I cry harder than I thought I could, gripping him in case he comes back again.

A week later, I can't stop staring at the huge rock pile next to the tiny one. Leo nudges me, he wants to go, but I can't. If I move away, Will's gone forever, again.

The snowflakes fall around me, trying to hide the rock pile from me.

I want to turn my back on them all, hike up into the woods, rebuild my cabin, and be alone again, but I promised him I would stay and keep them safe. Nothing has hurt as much as it does now. Now I love too much, hate too much, and hurt too much. Everything is bigger and they made it that way. I look up at the clouds covering the stars and whisper, "Meg." I don't need to tell her that I still need him. I don't need to tell her anything. She knows.

She knows me better than anyone.

I lean into Leo. He whines and readjusts. The cold ground hurts me too, but I block it out.

I hear footsteps on the cold, dry ground behind me. I don't need to turn to know it's Jake. His subtle limp is obvious if you listen well enough. He sits next to me, making warmth on that side.

"He asked me to give you something."

I stare at the rocks, hating him for accepting his death and giving up on me.

Jake presses something in my hand. I look down at the ring he placed there. It's a diamond ring with a silver-colored band.

"He wanted you to have it, even if he died. He was going to ask when he got better."

Tears fall from my eyes, landing on the diamond. His arm wraps around my body, but I don't move. I stare down at it. We sit in the snow for a long time, staring at the rock pile. I feel like my heart is buried under those rocks. The constant ache in my chest is too much to fight. I just let it own me.

I close my hand around the diamond ring and wonder when and where he got it from. I glance at Jake, "When did he get it?"

He closes his eyes, letting a single tear drip down his cheek. He whispers, "He traded his guitar for it at the camp, after you, Anna, and Star ran off without us."

I shake my head, "What?"

His eyes stay closed, "Yeah. One of the guys at the fire was saying he found a jewelry store that wasn't looted in a small town. He traded his guitar for it."

I grip it tighter.

"I hate him. Is that bad? I can't forgive him for leaving."

He shakes his head, "No. I hate him too." We cry silently, listening to the snow fall around us.

Chapter Seventeen

Two years later

I look at the rock pile and smile, "Meg, I think there's two kinds of love. One kind of love burns so hot that it burns out, before you get a chance to enjoy it. The other love is one that lifts you and makes you better than you were before." I grin and shake my head, "I know you always said Will was the right one for this world, but I think God knew better. Will was never the right choice, he was the only choice while he was here, but I don't know that it was better that way."

I look down at the diamond ring on my right hand as I brush the leaves off of the pile. The warmth of the spring sun is intense, as it always is. I don't confess my love for anyone; I just leave that thought out there and let her come to her own conclusions. I know she can see it all from where she is.

I cross my legs when I sit back down and ball a dried leave up, "So Anna and Nick; I bet you woulda seen that one coming. I never did, but you always saw more than me. The wedding tree has had four weddings under it now. Not sure if you were watching or not, but it was nice and it made the village brighten up for a few weeks." I look up into the sun and sigh, "I have to go, but I'll be back in a little while." Leo gets up with me and stretches. I run my hands through his fur and smile, "You're getting too old for these trips."

He gives me his annoyed look and saunters over to where Jake and Mitch are talking and pointing. I can see his hips are getting old. I am not sure what I'll do when he gets too old to be Leo anymore. I don't want to think about that.

Jake smiles when he sees me, "How's Meg?"

I shrug, "I think she gets lonely. I wish we could move her and the rose bush."

Jake shakes his head, "I like that she's here; I always think Bernie is too." His eyes are different than before. He nods at the horses, "Ready to go?"

I shrug, "Just waiting on you guys."

Mitch shakes his head, "If we let them put a trade market here, we will have more access to fruit. I think it's crazy to not do it."

Star walks from the back of the property, past all the charred rubble. It's her decision and they both know it.

She loops her arm into Mitch's, "Fine, but the rose bush and the grave are untouchable, and not negotiable."

Mitch smiles and kisses the side of her face, "I'll let them know. I'll meet you guys at the retreat?"

I glance up at Jake. He nods, "Yup. We just have to pick up Sarah and we're heading there."

I get on my horse and look down at Leo. He pants with his sloppy wolf face and starts towards the burned gates.

We ride slower, taking a little longer than normal. When we exit the forest, I smile. The village has grown in the two years we have been here. The log houses have taken over the old, dusty grass field and the forest has been cleared to make room for more houses. The white farmhouse is dirty but it's home to the cook pit ladies, Anna, and Nick. I can't sleep in there anymore. The smell of him is in there, even after we cleaned everything.

Sarah comes running up. She and Leo have their usual reunion. He lays down, looking tired. She gives me a look, "You have to make him stay. He can't do those big runs anymore."

I smile at the angry, little face, "Try telling him that."

She makes a noise and walks off with him. Jake laughs, "I think the teen years are about to hit."

I scowl at him, "She's twelve."

He shrugs, "Anna got evil at twelve."

I roll my eyes, "She was probably just tired of taking care of you."

He hops off his horse and drags me off of mine, "Oh really?" He throws me over his shoulder and carries me into the huge animal pen we've built for the cows, sheep, goats, and pigs. He tosses me into the haystack and jumps into the hay with me.

"Wanna roll in the hay?"

I shake my head, "No. It's prickly."

He pokes me in the arm, "You are getting softer. The Emma I met two years ago would have rolled in the hay, till it was soft as silk."

I snort.

He laughs, "I'm not kidding, you were like The Terminator."

I remember something and frown, "I'm pretty sure the last time you called me that, you also said I was a bitch and kissing me was a mistake."

His mouth hangs open for a second. He winces, "Yeah, that was the old me. I've improved, where as you've really slipped."

I smack his arm, "Shut up."

The hay pokes into my back, but I ignore it and glance over at him, "You ready to hike up?"

He nods, "I just want to tell you, kissing you was the first smart thing I ever did. Everything else from then on was insanely stupid."

"Not everything."

He laughs and gets up. I take his hand when he offers it and stand up.

We walk over to where Sarah is giving Leo water.

"Ready?"

She smiles, "I can't wait. First swim of the season."

Anna comes out of the farmhouse with her belly sticking out by a mile. I shake my head, "You look fatter than you did three days ago."

She flips me the bird. Nick comes out after her. His eyes are filled with worry. He's looked like that since she stopped getting her period again.

"The summer heat better wait for me to give birth, not even kidding."

Nick points, "We're heading over to the river for her to soak her feet again. The swelling is getting bad."

I look down and snicker at the tree stumps she has for ankles. She points, "You just wait. You'll have a baby one day and I'll make fun of your tree trunks too."

My face burns, but I shake my head, "I don’t think so."

Her eyes dart at Jake, "We'll see."

Jake and I have maintained our flirting, but he doesn’t know how I feel about him. Anna knows, because like Meg was able to, she can read my face perfectly. It's annoying.

We walk as a group to the river. The flow is higher with the snow melt so Anna and Nick stay in the area that is roped off with logs.

"Have fun swimming," she says with a sad face.

Nick growls at her, "We aren’t talking about this again. When the baby is born and healthy, we can talk about going to the retreat."

Anna sticks her tongue out at him. He's not like Bernie. He's like Will—a lot. He doesn’t take any shit off of her, which isn’t a bad thing. Jake loves him and the way he tells Anna like it is.

No one but Anna was happy she got pregnant again, least of all Nick. He and I both worry about what the baby will be. Things like me and him and Star have never reproduced before.

I wave to her, "Be safe, rest, and listen to Nick."

Nick winks at me, "You can say it all you want. She hears what she wants to."

Jake laughs and Anna swats Nick in the arm. He wraps himself around her, kissing her neck and whispering things to her. We leave them there, in love and happy. I wish I were more like her; I always have, but it's worse now. She is comfortable with her love for Bernie and Nick. She keeps them separate in her heart, but equally important.

When we get to the meeting tree, I stop in front of the rock pile I know is his. There are more now but his is directly under the meeting tree.

Jake and Sarah stand next to me. We are silent for a second and then Jake gives me a look, "Can you guys give me a minute?"

We nod and start up the hill to the left, to the retreat.

Sarah smiles at me with a funny glint in her eyes. I frown at her, "What did you do to him?"

She laughs, "What?"

I look back at Jake, "I see that look in your eyes. What have you been up to?"

She rolls her eyes, "For a smart girl, you are so dumb sometimes."

"Whatever." Great, the evil-teen years are coming.

We get pretty far ahead of Jake, but I don't worry as much about him. He doesn't walk quietly but he has learned to kill things.

I run my fingers through Leo's fur and grip my bow. Sarah grips hers too. She has become almost as good of a shot as some of the men. I think she'll be better at it than them in a couple years.

When I see the first guard in the platform, I wave. He waves back.

We crest the hill and see the people from the other camps and villages.

It's like a reunion every summer.

People wave and greet me with hugs and kindness. They ask about Anna and Nick, who like Star, has won them all over with his ability to be charming. They don't treat me the same way; there is still something in their eyes, but the death of Will and the fact I opened my home up to so many, has earned me a place.

It doesn't change the fact I am still awkward. Too many people around me makes me feel funny. They glance at my guns and my bow. I am one of the few allowed to bring weapons into the camps and villages, thanks to Star and her bright ideas. I fidget and think about Granny as we cross to the tents.

Abundance of food, smiles, and sunshine makes the retreat more fun.

People I recognize wave at me, women I saved hug me, and the ones who still think I'm the devil's mistress glare at me. For whatever reason, those people make me the most comfortable. Shit is wrong with me.

I walk through and head for the trail to the swimming hole. Sarah runs, stripping her clothes off.

Jake catches up, breathing heavily. He scowls when he sees Sarah stripping her outer shirt off, and looks like he's about to say something, but I laugh, "I told her she has to wear a shirt and shorts this year."

He sighs, "Thanks. Last year was awkward as ass."

Leo keeps up with Sarah. They dive into the water together. They still swim fairly similarly.

I pull off my tee shirt, shorts, my gun holsters, knife in my boots, and quiver and bow. Jake looks at the pile and shakes his head. I scowl and jump in, in my underwear and tank top.

The water is cold; I gasp and try to catch my breath. It's the cleanest I've felt all year. I splash around, enjoying the cool of the water when my body adjusts. I look over at Jake, seeing the large, lumpy scar on his leg.

He dives in and swims underwater to where I am. It makes me

nervous. He always pulls me under when we swim; I hate it.

Instead, he surfaces close to my face and spits water at me. Sarah laughs. I leap at him, dunking him under the water for a change.

He laughs and pulls me under.

Sarah starts to shiver. She nods at me, "I'm going to find Nan and get something to eat."

Jake points at her, "You stay with the cook hags. You do not walk around until we get up there."

She rolls her eyes and swims away. I look at Leo, "Stay with Sarah."

He almost rolls his eyes too and splashes after her. He jumps out, shaking his body and covering our clothes in water. Jake sighs, "That wolf is a vindictive bastard."

I nod, "Yeah," and lay back to float, looking up at the clouds.

I feel him float over near to me.

"Tell me something you remember from before."

"One time, when I was about ten or eleven my mom and dad took us to this restaurant. It was really fancy and expensive. Mom got a promotion and we were celebrating it. I had to go to the bathroom; I spilled some of the sauce from my steak on my pants. Dad laughed but mom was mad. I went to clean up and there was a guy in there. He had on a suit and a nervous look. He was pacing. He freaked me out a little bit. He pulled a box out of his suit pocket and sighed looking at this huge diamond ring. He saw me looking and held it so I could see too. He asked me if I thought it was nice. I said yeah, I didn’t really know if it was or not. He took a deep breath and nodded his head and said, wish me luck kid. So I said good luck and he walked out. When I finished washing my pants off and drying them under the hand dryer, I got out into the restaurant and he was on his knee. A pretty lady was crying and nodding. The whole restaurant starting clapping as he slid the ring on her finger. He and the lady hugged and kissed, and my mom cried a little bit. She and Dad leaned in and kissed too." He laughs, "I remember thinking that was exactly how I would ask my wife to marry me."

I smile and look over at him. He's not floating on his back, he's holding something and treading water next to me.

The thing in his hands is a metal box, rough and rusted. He opens it and inside is a ring with a red stone. It looks like a ring I once gave to Stella as payment to escape with my life and virtue intact.

I look into his eyes, seeing the sparkle that was there before I made him more like me.

He grins, "I don't have a fancy restaurant to take you to, and even if I did, I'm not sure you would like it. Your fondness for killing the things you eat is not something that would have suited that. And honestly, I can't think of a better place to tell you I love you. Even when I shouldn't have, and I wasn't supposed to, I did. I wanted you when I met you and I still do. I can't change the way I feel, so I am embracing it. If you need more time…"

I swim to him, cutting him off and wrap my legs around him. I place my hands on his face, close my eyes, and press my lips to his.

His body against mine is warm and comfortable. His love is the kind that makes my heart safe. My mind tries to compare them, but my heart stops and makes room for them both. Anna was right, there is no time. Today could be all I get and I don't want to be without him for one minute longer.

I feel tears streaming my face, "I love you too. Even when I wasn't supposed to and I shouldn't have, I did."

He nods, "And we both still love him and I think that's okay."

I nod into his face and pray to God that I get more. More days and more love and more happiness.

Epilogue

Ten years ago, I made a choice to save a girl and she ended up saving me in the end.

Ten years ago, I killed the man who took everything from me. The man who killed my real dad.

Ten years ago, I realized my mother was a good person.

Ten years ago, I fell in love with a man I hated as much as I loved. A man as damaged as me. I like to think we healed each other as much as we hurt each other.

Ten years ago, I fell in love with another man, one who made me happy in a way I tried to fight, because he was everything I didn't think I deserved.

Today, as I look down on him sleeping next to me, I can't help but think how perfect we are for each other. He makes me soft and I make him strong and together we accept the love we both still have for his brother.

"Auntie Em!"

I roll over as the twins attack.

"Uncle Jake!"

He moans and tries to pull his pillow over his face, "Uncle Jake needs sleep."

I laugh and hug Meg to me. She squeals and curls into my body. She bats her blue-green eyes that look remarkably like mine. She peers at me through her lashes, "What did you get me for my birthday?"

I roll my eyes, "It can't be your birthday already."

Bernard frowns, "It is, Aunty Em."

Jake looks puzzled, "How many is it this year?"

Bernard rolls his blue-green eyes, "Seven. We told you this yesterday and Momma says you have to get up. We can't have cake without you."

I rub his brown hair that looks like his uncle's, "Bernie, why don't you and Meg go look in the drawer over there." I point at the dresser Jake made. It's a little crooked, but I like it that way.

They hop off and run for the drawer. Meg squeals in delight as she pulls the bow and quiver from the drawer. She looks back, "Really?"

I nod, "Go see Sarah. She'll help you make arrows and teach you to shoot it, and tell you the rules."

She gushes, "I hope I'm as good of a hunter as she is, well, one day."

Bernard doesn't look as excited about the matching bows and quivers. Jake laughs and points at the second drawer, "Check that one out."

He opens it and freezes. His jaw drops and when he looks at us it makes me smile harder. "Robin Hood?" He lifts the book out of the drawer and holds it to his chest. Meg makes a face and runs out of the house, no doubt in search of Sarah. Bernard cracks the book open and walks out of the house, dragging the bow behind him.

Jake looks at me with so much love in his eyes. Sometimes I wonder if he's sad that I can't have a baby. The one time I asked him he got angry; he never really does that much.

"It's weird they are exactly like their namesakes."

I laugh, "I know. Meg is a savage and Bernie is a bookworm."

He glances at me, "At least Will is nothing like Will."

I roll my eyes, "Poor girl, who saddles a four year old with the name Will?"

He wraps himself around me, "I wonder what Star and Mitch got the twins? Can't be as cool as our gift."

I sigh, "We rode a long ways to find that book."

Anna comes in the house seconds later, "Get up. Jeeze. You're worse than the teenagers."

Jake moans, "We were on watch last night, Anna."

She snorts, "Did you know Star gave them their own sheriff badges? Will is out there trying to steal Bernie's. I can't believe you gave them a weapon and she gave them badges to make those weapons lawful."

I look at Jake, "Oh, that's cooler than our gift."

He points, "Only to Meg."

Anna sighs, "You going to the trade market tomorrow?"

I nod, "Yeah. I need to see him."

She nods, "I'm coming." She gives Jake a sweet look and bats her eyelashes, "Can you stay here and help Nick with the twins?"

He smiles, "Yeah. I can help Sarah teach Meg not to shoot other people."

As a village we celebrate their birthday, the first babies born here. We laugh, joke and eat. It's a night filled with dancing and singing.

We have learned to make joy and live every day.

Nothing is perfect but it's better.

Outlaws are gunned down by the sheriffs Star and Mitch run. Criminals are punished harshly. Trade markets no longer trade people. Brothels are the new way of keeping women down, but Star burns them when she finds them. She has learned to use her anger and hatred in a good way. Sometimes I ride with her to release my inner demons.

Nothing is ever going to be perfect. I still haven't found all the people Marshall was with; the bad people who kill kids like me.

When I stumble upon them I kill them, but I know there are more. There always will be bad people. The kids Michael made have blended. We don't see packs of them like we did in the city. Society has either killed them or accepted them, depending on where they ended up and their behavior.

Anna and I ride into the trade market the next day. The smell of fruit is everywhere. The warm summer months make the trade market the best place to come. There is fruit, baking, and roasting everywhere.

We ride past the market though, heading for the place that was never part of the deal for the land.

I get off of my horse and tie him to a post. Anna and I walk to the two rock piles under the rose bush that seems so large now, I hardly recognize it. Anna picks the leaves and sticks off of the headstone that was placed here with Bernie's name on it.

I drop in front of the one I buried him under two summers ago. He had to have been the oldest-lived wolf ever.

I place the stone from my pocket in the pile and just let the tears come.

"I miss you, buddy."

He died old, fat, and happy. He died sleeping next to a warm dish of food. If anyone deserved that death it was him.

I look up at the sky and smile, "You all hug each other for me."

Anna and I still cry every time we come. Sarah refuses to come. She won't see him in the ground.

Someone once told me to find another timber wolf for a pet. They didn't understand he was never my pet. He was my family. He was the warmth in the dark and the person I needed to not be alone.

No one but Anna, Sarah, and Jake can understand the value of Leo. He was family.

Anna grips my hand and I try to smile. "I wish he could have lived forever."

Anna nods and sniffles, "Me too."

I look down at the spot on my skin, where I had the smithy burn his name into my arm, and rub the scar.

I look at Anna and know Leo led them to me. I like to think that he knew one day he would be gone and I would be alone. He found a family for me. He chose them and I don't think anyone could have chosen better.

Through the thick and thin, and the good and the bad, no one but Leo could have found me a better place to fit in or better people.

No one knew me the way Leo did.

I believe in God because of the two people in front of me—Meg and Leo, angels in disguise.

There are a thousand things I could have changed and made different than they are now, but then maybe I wouldn't have the life I do. Everyday there is more. More love, more happiness, and more gratitude for everyday I wake up free.

They say that the world was built for two. I used to doubt that and think that two was a long lost dream. I used to believe we didn't deserve the happiness of the perfect place we all remembered.

But that world wasn't ever real; it never existed. It was a daydream and a memory we made up. We didn't want the change, but in some ways we needed it.

Some things were easier before, but almost everything is better now.

Nothing is instant; evil and hatred take time. It isn't as easy as using the internet to make hate, or commit crimes from a speeding car with a gun out the window. Everything takes time and effort. The good and the bad.

I see now that true love isn't fickle; it's what we put into it. If we work hard at loving someone, then no one can corrupt the love we have.

I see everything differently than before and I have Leo to thank for that.

I wasn’t born into this world. I had to learn how to survive and live with the other people in it. But like Jake always says, I was raised by wolves, so I had to expect it was going to be hard to learn how to fit in.

Looking back on it all, I can't think of a better way to be raised than by a wolf, and I can't think of a better wolf to raise a savage little girl all on his own.

I lift the rock I found, with the pretty crystals in it, to my lips and kiss it. The warmth of the stone against my lips is a comfort. I place it back down on the pile and hold my hand there, "I love you both."

I get up and walk away, holding the hand of my sister, grateful for my ‘us’. Because it's us and them, it always was.

The End

Thank you for being part of my US

ABOUT THE AUTHOR

Tara Brown is a Canadian author who writes Fantasy, Science Fiction, Paranormal Romance and Contemporary Romance in New Adult, Young Adult and Adult fiction. She lives in Eastern Canada with her husband, two daughters and pets.

Other Books by Tara Brown

The Devil's Roses

Cursed

Bane

Witch

Hyde

Death

The Born Trilogy

Born

Born to Fight

The Light Series

The Light of the World

Imaginations

The Blood Trail Chronicles

Vengeance

Blackwater Witches

Blackwater

The Single Lady Spy Series

The End of Me

My Side

The Long Way Home

The Lonely

P.I.'s Like Us

LOST BOY